THE BOXTROLLS ™

Copyright © 2014 by Universal Studios Licensing LLC.
The Boxtrolls ™ © 2013 Boxtrolls LLC.
Licensed by Universal Studios Licensing LLC.
All rights reserved.

Little, Brown and Company

Hachette Book Group
237 Park Avenue, New York, NY 10017
Visit us at lb-kids.com

Little, Brown and Company is a division
of Hachette Book Group, Inc.
The Little, Brown name and logo are trademarks
of Hachette Book Group, Inc.

The publisher is not responsible for websites (or their content)
that are not owned by the publisher.

First Edition: September 2014

ISBN 978-0-316-33264-4

Library of Congress Control Number: 2014939547

10 9 8 7 6 5 4 3 2 1

RRD-C

Printed in the United States of America

THE BOXTROLLS

A Novel

by Elizabeth Cody Kimmel

Screenplay by IRENA BRIGNULL & ADAM PAVA

Based upon the book *Here Be Monsters!* by ALAN SNOW

Little, Brown and Company
New York Boston

For Jackson Hummer, who sometimes likes cheese, and sometimes does not.

Prologue

Winifred Portley-Rind made a point of taking a very long walk every afternoon down the narrow, steep streets of Cheesebridge. She called it her "daily constitutional" and claimed it was for her health. But actually, eleven-year-old Winnie was bored. School was moderately uninteresting, and home was excessively tedious. Winnie's father was Cheesebridge's leading citizen, which made him excruciatingly dull. And Winnie's mother was obsessed with clothes, clothes, and more clothes—an outfit for virtually every hour of the day—and that, of course, was colossally tiresome. And so the daily constitutional was born, and Winnie escaped the monotony for several hours. There was only one problem with her strategy: The village of Cheesebridge was pretty humdrum itself.

In fact, as every man, woman, and child knew, there were 364 perfectly normal days in Cheesebridge each and every year. And then there was Trubshaw Baby Day. Now, *that* day was anything but dull.

Along the narrow sidewalk of Buttery Street, most merchants had some sort of sign or banner counting down to Trubshaw Baby Day. As Winnie strolled past the Wheel of Fortune gift shop, a freshly spruced-up flag fluttered in the wind, announcing ONLY 3 DAYS TO TBD!

Three days, Winnie thought. And then the town would come to life. There would be parades, special performers, feasts, bonfires, theatrics, fireworks, raffles, and a gala ball. All to solemnly commemorate the gruesome day almost ten years ago when the little Trubshaw baby disappeared and presumably was killed by creatures that lived underneath Cheesebridge. The Boxtrolls.

The mazelike streets and alleys, along which sat high, narrow homes and shops, were all closely packed together. Even on a long walk, one could get only so far.

"Good afternoon, Miss Portley-Rind!" called a waiter from the doorway of Chez Fromage, one of the town's fancier restaurants.

"Good morning, Jean-Louise," Winnie replied.

"Only three days to go. Are you excited?" Jean-Louise asked.

"Wildly excited, to say the least," Winnie called over her shoulder as she continued to walk.

And it was true—Winnie was excited. But not as much as she'd been last year, and again the year before that. Because, having lived through exactly nine Trubshaw Baby Days so far (the first two or three were a bit of a blur), she found that some of the thrill had recently gone out of it. Winnie wasn't quite sure why. It seemed to be a combination of things.

For starters, Winnie had begun to wonder why a day commemorating a tragic abduction and murder was the subject of celebration.

Maybe I'm just strange, Winnie thought, *but when I think about the tragic loss of a tiny baby, the first things that come to mind aren't dancing, feasting, parading, souvenir hawking, or general all-out partying.*

Yes, that was probably part of the problem, Winnie decided. But there was more to it than that. And the older she got, the more she felt it. Winnie wasn't just bored with her life. She was, in fact, aching for some excitement, for something different, for some real-life danger. For as long as Winnie could remember, there had been a curfew in Cheesebridge. After darkness had fallen each night, shops were closed down and people retreated to their homes, where they triple-locked their doors and shuttered their windows. The things that had taken the Trubshaw baby, as everyone knew, came out of their Death Cave only at night, to roam the streets in search of fresh victims. And that sounded excessively dangerous, to be sure.

However, after the Trubshaw baby, no one else of note had disappeared from Cheesebridge. The man taking credit for that was the creepily repulsive Archibald Snatcher, who patrolled the streets with his team of three Red Hats (so named for the red hats they almost never took off). Snatcher said his patrol was so intimidating that the monsters had been forced to hunt in other towns. In short, Snatcher had made commuters out of them. Whenever they did appear in Cheesebridge—and there were people who claimed to have seen them—the Red Hats pursued them and either exterminated them or drove them back to their Death Cave.

But in almost ten years, you'd think the monsters would have killed at least one other Cheesebridgian,

Winnie mused. *Or, I don't know…taken a few bites out of one.*

And yet she could not think of another person who had gone missing. It wasn't that she didn't believe in the monsters—she most certainly did. She had been taught all about them, and about the Trubshaw baby, for years, both at school and at home. Adults didn't make up things like that. No, the monsters were very real.

So the only explanation, Winnie decided, *is that Snatcher is right, and whenever the monsters come looking for a meal in Cheesebridge, the Red Hats take care of the situation before any violence can occur.*

Winnie knew she ought to be thankful for that. Snatcher certainly made no secret of his belief that every man, woman, and child should spend the better part of each day being thankful for the protection and vigilance of Archibald P. Snatcher.

But as Winnie's curls bounced past yet another cheese shop, she knew that all calm and no murder made Cheesebridge a dull town. There had to be more to life than the Cheese Guild, and getting cheese or tasting cheese or hearing about cheese. There had to be something beyond the countdown to Trubshaw Baby Day, and Winnie's daily constitutional.

One day when I'm old enough, I'll travel, Winnie told herself. *I'll leave Cheesebridge and see the sights, have some adventures, live dangerously. I'll be a fearless explorer and battle monsters and save people from awful things, and everyone will love me. And I'll wear the same thing every day and I won't ever have to put on another itchy dress or frilly shirt with puffed sleeves, not for the rest of my life.*

The thought of it made Winnie feel a little better. But only a little. She knew she was still only a kid. It would be a long time before she was old enough to pack up and begin her travels.

But I'll do it, she silently promised. *Because there has to be something else out there, something different, something totally unknown. And I'm going to find it, even if I have to travel halfway across the world.*

Winnie tripped over something and almost fell.

"Darn it!" she exclaimed.

In the midst of her daydreaming, she had absent-mindedly wandered from the sidewalk and into the street. She looked down and saw she had just caught her foot on the lip of a manhole cover that was ever so slightly dislodged.

I must be more careful, she told herself. *I don't want to get run over by a truck before I've so much as gotten a toe near some place other than Cheesebridge.*

Winnie stepped back onto the sidewalk and picked up her pace a little. Seconds later, when there was a quick clanking noise and the manhole cover suddenly dropped back into place, Winnie was too far away to hear it, or to notice anything out of the ordinary happening where she had just been standing.

Something had moved it from below.

Chapter 1

The world had been divided into Aboveground and Belowground for as long as Eggs could remember. It was just the way of things. Aboveground, different creatures lived in wooden things called houses, on a hill crammed with wooden things and flat paths. All the wooden things and paths and creatures together were called Cheesebridge. The creatures were called people.

People wore flappy bits with ruffles and stripes, but Boxtrolls dressed themselves in sturdy boxes. Eggs loved his own box with a picture of an egg on the front. You only needed one good box.

Belowground, Eggs lived happily with the other Boxtrolls. When the cheese people were awake, the Boxtrolls slept. And when the cheese people slept, the Boxtrolls made their way to the surface and combed the streets and garbage bins for junky-bits—anything useful that could be made into a gizmo or a machine or a contraption. The Boxtrolls found the most wonderful things Aboveground—it was amazing to Eggs that any creature with a working brain would want to throw such treasures away.

From his cozy cavern nook, Eggs could see countless junky-bits: findsies and shinies, clunkers, honkers, and spinners. Almost all of them found their way into an invention or a motor or a thingamajig; there was nothing Eggs's friends couldn't make or fix or fudge together.

Eggs himself was partial to musical machines. Of course, the entire cavern was filled with music of one kind or another: the smooth *wah-wah-wah* of the waterwheel that provided electricity, the *clackity-clackity-squeal* of the troll-lift that sounded like a soprano warming up for the opera, and the occasional baritone hum of the conveyor belt that delivered Boxtrolls safely home after an evening of junky-bits hunting Aboveground.

In the garden, oversized, sweet-tempered Fragile was working one side of a seesaw pump, while shrimpy, bossy Bucket worked the other. Bucket had a strange box that covered the back and sides of his head, giving him the appearance of a turtle in a coffin. When Bucket and Fragile got the pump working, it made a steady *hee-haw* like an overexcited donkey. Water dripped into hanging umbrellas, and from there, small drops funneled to the ground, neatly splattering, to sate thirsty vegetables. Put together, the sounds made a little song that Eggs liked to hum along to: *hee-HAW plink plink, hee-HAW plink plink, hee-HAW plinkety plink, kersplat.* Then the whole thing started over again.

At the other end of the cave, the conveyor belt began to move, the hundreds of tin cans that acted as rollers all rattling together. Eggs sat up. Someone was returning home!

Eggs never failed to feel a rush of excitement when the Boxtrolls came back after a night of junky-bits hunting. They sometimes brought extraordinary and fascinating things from Aboveground. Eggs wished with all his heart that he could go with them. Not a day passed when he didn't hope Fish would place a giant hand on his shoulder and guide him into the Sucker-Upper with the others.

They think I'm too young. They all do, Eggs thought

ruefully. *And I'm not! Maybe I was for a while....*

And Shoe had given Eggs three pairs of sneakers this year, and they just kept ending up too small. So something was happening. And yet Eggs knew that next to the other Boxtrolls, even little, timid Knickers, he still looked pretty puny. Unlike the others', Eggs's head fur was thick and shiny, not coarse and wiry and in one small tuft as it should have been. For as long as he could remember, Eggs had suffered from an irritation of the skin that left him a peculiar shade of pale peach all over, rather than a healthy gray or a robust green. His fingers were not the least bit sausage-like; instead, they were alarmingly slender and delicate. To add insult to injury, Eggs had also been born with ears that did not taper into little points in the regular way. They were round and dainty, like two little seashells. Eggs was particularly sensitive about them. To complete the picture, Eggs had small, unmistakably brown eyes. Though he sometimes imagined they contained a hint of yellow in a certain light, he knew he was kidding himself. And no matter how hard he tried, he simply could not make his eyes glow golden amber in the dark, when every other Boxtroll in the world was born knowing how to do it.

There was no getting around it. Eggs was the weirdest-looking Boxtroll in the cave.

But weird-looking doesn't mean I'm not getting older, Eggs told himself.

Now Eggs could hear the *swish-swish* of a Boxtroll careening down the cardboard-lined chute to the conveyor belt. Maybe it was Fish or Shoe with a new part for his Music Machine! Fish dropped onto the conveyor belt and was carried down to the cave floor, where he landed on a pillow with a dignified *thunk*. Moments later, Shoe shot out of the chute, and the belt deposited him on the pillow next to Fish.

"Did you find something for me?" Eggs called out excitedly.

Fish's face lit up at the sound of Eggs's voice, and his smile revealed his perfectly yellow and divinely pointy teeth. He stood up and brushed off his box as he stretched his long legs and scratched his lovely potato-shaped head. Fish was quite tall for a Boxtroll. When Shoe stood up glowering next to him, he looked like a hostile toadstool. Fish chattered away in his usual stream of gurgles and rummaged around in his box as Eggs nodded patiently. Finally, Fish produced a small, round object and handed it to Eggs.

"Oh, a rubbery grommet!" Eggs exclaimed. "This could be just the thing I need for my Music Machine. Thank you, Fish."

Fish burbled something that meant "You're welcome" as Shoe began rummaging around in *his* box. Eggs watched with curiosity and more than a little wistful envy. Shoe always found good things, but often he liked to hide anything that gleamed or glittered. If you had a shiny and Shoe was around, you had to keep your eye on him. Shinies (and nuts of most varieties) had a way of accidentally sneaking into Shoe's box.

"Soon I will be old enough to go Aboveground and hunt for junky-bits," Eggs declared.

Fish and Shoe exchanged a look with twin pairs of unblinking yellow eyes.

"Well, I will," Eggs repeated more quietly, turning away to retrieve his Music Machine and work in the addition of the rubbery grommet.

"*Glerbug blime*," Fish stated, and Shoe joined in with an enthusiastic "*Gerblug!*"

"Now that you mention it, I am kind of hungry," Eggs agreed. The conveyor belt had started up again, and more Boxtrolls were beginning to arrive. Soon they would all be home.

Definitely best to eat early, Eggs thought. In this cave, the early bird really did get the worm.

Eggs followed Fish and Shoe to the Garden of Wriggly Delights. Fragile and Bucket were taking a break from the pump and were sitting in the grass, looking for snacks. The garden's lush and abundant plantings provided for all of the Boxtrolls' nutritional needs. There were juicy bumper worms and tart fatty-grubs in the soil, crunchy winger-zingers (if you could catch one) zooming from umbrella to umbrella, candy-colored scootcher beetles lounging under leaves, and gazillipedes scuttling underfoot—you had to be fast to eat them or they would climb back out of your mouth.

"Gluvrrooooom!" someone yelled, and Eggs jumped to one side as Wheels sped by on the unicycle he rode everywhere, serenading himself with a selection of burbled engine noises. Knickers tottered in next, followed by a tall, quiet Boxtroll named Sparky, wearing his customary welding goggles. Knickers's small size and wide-set, anxious expression made him look like a nervously dazed piglet. Eggs held out the rubbery grommet, and Sparky flipped up his goggles to examine it. He made a *glubbedy-goo* of delight and nodded

approvingly. Knickers shifted from foot to foot nervously, breathing loudly through his mouth.

"Wanna see it, Knickers?" Eggs asked, holding out the grommet. Knickers shrieked and jumped back as if Eggs had threatened him with a freshly sharpened ax.

"*Gloggown,*" Fish said, patting a nice mound of earth. Eggs smiled. He could always count on Fish to save him the best seat. Fish rooted around in the soil with his clawlike nails, unearthing a pale pink bumper worm that wriggled in protest. With his other hand, Fish produced a nut from an earthen hole and placed it on the ground, beaming at Eggs from ear to ear. Shoe appeared out of nowhere, tapping the back of Fish's arm and then reaching for the nut when Fish turned his head.

"*Burblop!*" Fish yelled, slapping Shoe's hand away. Fish picked up the worm, tied it neatly around the nut, then handed the undulating delicacy to Eggs.

"*Gloo,*" Fish said, nodding approvingly as Eggs popped the whole concoction into his mouth. Shoe ambled away, making muttering sounds under his breath.

"*Gavooom!*" Wheels shouted excitedly, holding a huge gazillipede by a few hundred of its legs. He waved triumphantly at Eggs, then leaned his head back and carefully lowered the insect down his throat in the manner of a sword-swallower. By the pump, Eggs could hear Sparky and Knickers having some kind of dispute over a winger-zinger. They stood facing each other, each holding one of the zinger's wings. Sparky's usually expressionless face was pinched, as if he might cry, but he let loose a massive sneeze instead, giving poor Knickers such a fright that he dove into his own box for cover. When Sparky saw that Eggs was watching, he winked, held up the zinger by one wing, and popped it into his mouth, chewing with great relish. Eggs smiled back, looking around as other Boxtrolls came in to dine. Books was over by the shrubs, doing a little digging. When he stood up, he handed two butter-soft fatty-grubs to old Sweets, who popped out his false teeth and bobbed his head in gratitude. Only after Sweets had eaten both of the fatty-grubs did Books sit down to eat his own dinner—a handful of scootcher beetles—which he consumed while flipping through a tattered copy of *For Whom the Box Trolls*.

Shoe reappeared, plopping down next to Eggs and dumping a handful of nuts and several bottle caps on the ground. He tossed a nut into his mouth and waggled his eyebrows at Eggs, who laughed.

"How did you find all those nuts so fast?" Eggs asked. "Did you swipe them from somebody?"

Shoe did his best to look morally outraged at the suggestion of theft as he put a second nut in his mouth, holding one in each cheek like a chipmunk with hoarding issues.

"I meant what I said before, you know," Eggs said, looking from Shoe to Fish. "I will be old enough soon to go Aboveground to hunt for junky-bits. I'm probably already old enough."

Fish and Shoe exchanged a brief look. Eggs sighed.

Fish and Shoe were probably thinking about what had happened the first and only time Eggs had ventured Aboveground. Eggs thought about it, too. In fact, he thought about it a great deal. He hadn't *really* gone Aboveground—not technically, because his feet had stayed underground the entire time. But Eggs's whole head, including his eyes, had been Aboveground, and the manhole cover had been pushed aside just enough to give him a very good view of the street.

Eggs did not like what he saw that day. And he most definitely did not like what he heard. He ran the whole miserable scene through his head again.

First, there was a voice that sounded like it was coming out of some different kind of Music Machine, maybe one that had a few too many rubbery grommets.

"Hear ye! Hear ye! Hear ye!" the voice bellowed, and Eggs put his hands over his ears, which were small and delicate and accustomed to gentle Boxtroll burbles and gurgles.

"Take heed, take heed!" the voice continued. "All must be off the streets: The curfew is now in force! The day is done, the night is nigh! All off the streets, Cheesebridgians!"

That sounded pretty peculiar to Eggs. Why leave the streets at night? That was the time when all the best things happened. Dark was the time for junky-bits hunting—the night was filled with gears and springs and widgets just waiting to be found by a Boxtroll, so they could be made into something marvelous for the cavern. Why would the Cheese Bits want to clear the street?

Eggs felt the cobblestones around the manhole vibrate slightly, and he heard the unmistakable hum of an engine. Boxtrolls knew engines, any kind, all kinds. The voice blared again, louder this time.

"Good citizens of Cheesebridge, do not be caught out in the dark, where the horrid monsters roam. Now is not the time for bravery or foolishness! Leave that to us."

Monsters? Roaming the Cheese Bits' streets? Eggs blinked in surprise. This was certainly the first *he'd* ever heard of it. The hum and growl grew louder, and Eggs drew slightly back as a funny boxy thing on wheels rattled into view, a lumpy load of furniture and bags mounted precariously on the roof. Two sinister-looking creatures of differing shapes and sizes, wearing stovepipe hats of blood red, clung to the side of the vehicle. One of them was gigantic, a bald-headed creature almost spilling out of his clothes, his red hat freakishly tiny on his colossal and slightly misshapen head. The second man was long and lean like a bit of taffy that had been pulled end from end. His head seemed too small for the rest of him, save for his oversized ears, which stuck out at such an odd angle, it seemed they were trying to escape. And now Eggs realized that what he had mistaken for a lumpy load strapped to the roof was actually another Red Hat, clutching one arm of the chair and pursing his lips as he looked around.

Those must be some of the Cheese Bit creatures, Eggs thought. *Aren't they just awful-looking! Exceptionally ugly. Some of them look like overgrown fatty-grubs.* Little wonder his friends had always tried to keep him from seeing them. But Eggs was getting older now. And not all Boxtrolls were big and strong. Sweet little Oil Can, who had always had a dollop of oil at the ready for any gizmo that needed it, was quite small, and the high-strung Knickers wasn't much bigger. No, Eggs really believed he was ready for this sort of thing now, even if the Cheese Bits were an ugly bit of business.

The boxy vehicle was passing by now, just yards from where Eggs peered wide-eyed in his hiding place. Now Eggs could see there were letters painted on the side. Books had gone to a great deal of trouble to teach Eggs his letters, and Eggs had done his best to pay attention, though the whole thing seemed rather point-less. But now he tried to make out what the words on the boxy thing said.

"Buh-ah-zzz tuh-ruh-oh-ss. Buzz tross?" Eggs worked the sounds around in his mouth. "Boxtrolls!"

he exclaimed triumphantly. Boy, wouldn't Books be impressed when Eggs told him about reading that!

The second word proved a little more challenging.

"Eh-k-s," he said. "Eggs! That's me! Eggs-tuh-er-my-nah-tore. Eggs…"

Wait. Eggs knew this word, because it was written on the side of a big plastic jug he'd once tried to incorporate into his Music Machine, along with a drawing of a big dead bug.

Exterminator.

Boxtroll exterminators.

Eggs didn't get the chance to savor his triumph of phonics, because the meaning suddenly became clear to him.

"Boxtroll exterminators? The Cheese Bits exterminate *us*?"

As the boxy thing neared, Eggs could see its driver. His lips were pulled back in a snarl, his buggy eyes huge behind a pair of round spectacles. Perched atop his egg-shaped head was a tattered red hat that was every bit as twisted and grizzled as his face. As if some silent signal had been given, the Red Hat's head snapped to the left, his cold eyes fixed directly on Eggs. The man looked as if he might eat Eggs for breakfast and not think any-thing of it.

Eggs smacked one small hand over his mouth in horror. Why would the red-hatted Cheese Bits hunt Boxtrolls? That certainly wasn't very *neighborly* of them.

As the vehicle slowly pulled away, Eggs realized the voice he'd heard belonged to the reptilian-looking Red Hat sitting on top. He held a funnel-shaped device to his mouth as he spoke.

"Lock your doors, bolt your windows!" the Red Hat called. "Fathers, hide your mechanicals! Mothers, hug your children! Keep them safe from the vicious beasts of the night!"

Vicious beasts? Eggs wondered. *I suppose he means me, and Fish, and Shoe, and everyone. How rude.*

A small Cheese Bit began to run alongside the truck.

"How many monsters will you catch tonight, Mr. Snatcher?" the little Bit shouted.

"Child, do you want to end up like the Trubshaw baby? Snatched away in the deadly shadows? Eaten alive in an underground cave? Your poor father searching for you into the night?" the man yelled.

The small Cheese Bit came to an abrupt stop.

"No one wants to end up like the Trubshaw baby," the boy mumbled, looking nervously around as the boxy vehicle drove away, the one called Snatcher still droning his warnings.

When the street was clear at last, Eggs pulled the manhole cover back into place and scurried down to the safety of the Boxtroll cavern. When the other Boxtrolls returned later, sweet little Oil Can was not with them. Boxtrolls did go away sometimes; Eggs had known that. But he had always thought they had just decided to move somewhere else. But the day Eggs peeked Aboveground was the day he realized that when the Boxtrolls went hunting junky-bits, something else went hunting *them*. And they didn't always come back.

He hadn't been Aboveground since. All the fun had been taken out of it.

Nevertheless, Eggs knew in his heart he was getting to be the age when he ought to be joining his fellow Boxtrolls on their nightly junky-bits hunt.

I want to help gather gizmos and findsies for the cavern, Eggs thought. *I won't let any grubby Cheese Bit exterminate me.*

Fish and Shoe were burbling quietly to each other but fell silent when they saw Eggs watching them. Eggs suddenly got the idea maybe they had been talking about *him*.

"Look, I mean it. I am ready to start going Aboveground with the rest of you," Eggs said loudly.

Shoe fidgeted inside his box. His head disappeared for a moment, then reappeared. He waddled over to Eggs and handed him something, then walked away before Eggs had a chance to say anything.

Eggs unwrapped the object Shoe had handed him. It was a pair of new shoes. They were yellow and had teddy bears drawn on them. Eggs sighed.

But they're wrong about me, Eggs told himself. *Just because I happen to have a few physical flaws, through absolutely no fault of my own, doesn't mean I can't hold my own Aboveground.*

In the center of the cavern, the Boxtrolls had begun the process of stacking themselves one on top of another in the traditional Boxtroll sleeping pile.

Eggs stifled a yawn. He wanted to give a speech right then and make everyone take notice. Fish, Shoe, Books, Bucket, all of them. They would all hear him standing up for himself and be impressed with his moxie. They would agree it was time for Eggs to join the pack. But it was getting early, and the sleeping pile looked tantalizing, indeed.

That's all right. I'll go to sleep now like everyone else, Eggs thought. He adjusted his box, then began to climb to the top of the sleeping pile. He kept his head down so the other Boxtrolls wouldn't notice the big smile on his face. They would just think *that* was weird, too. But it didn't matter.

Come the next night, Eggs would take his rightful place Aboveground, shoulder-to-shoulder with his fellow Boxtrolls.

Chapter 2

In the end, for reasons Eggs could not figure out, the Boxtrolls relented the following night, as if his first trip Aboveground had been on the calendar for months. Eggs was gearing up to give his nightly speech when Fish appeared silently at his side. He gave Eggs a long hug, practically flattening his box in the process, then handed him a gizmo that looked like a helmet with shiny bits. Eggs put it on. It was a cap fashioned out of leather and what Eggs thought were windows on top, until Fish flipped them down over Eggs's eyes and switched them on. The gathered Boxtrolls burbled and drummed their boxes with approval as Eggs grinned from ear to ear. His funny eyes might not glow yellow in the dark, but with this gizmo, Eggs would be able to do anything the other Boxtrolls could.

Fish gave him a gentle push to the Sucker-Upper, which whisked Boxtrolls from the cave toward the surface. Too surprised to say anything, and afraid Fish would change his mind, Eggs stepped under the Sucker-Upper and scrunched his face at the powerful sensation of indrawn air that gulped him upward as if he were a bit of lemonade in a straw. It made his insides feel squishy and his ears all tickly, but Eggs didn't care. He was Aboveground! He waited, humming with excitement, as the Boxtrolls burbled. Knickers, Clocks, and Sparky were going to investigate some kind of alley, from what Eggs could gather. Eggs was to go with Fish, Shoe, and Wheels toward a wooden house surrounded by shrubs and garden ornaments. Every window blazed with light.

Fish showed Eggs how to walk quietly, keeping his head low. He made him practice Emergency Boxing a few times. You had to drop to the ground and pull your legs, arms, and head inside your box. Then, to any passing eye, you were just an old bit of cardboard. Eggs's box was even smaller than it had been last month, but he finally executed an Emergency Boxing that passed Fish's inspection.

Fish led Eggs toward the house, one huge hand gently but firmly gripping Eggs's box. There were several large, round cans in front of the house. Shoe and

Wheels had already reached one of them and were digging through it, their yellow eyes gleaming brightly.

Fish was standing beneath the window. He pointed at his own head, then dropped into his box. Eggs climbed on top of him and peered through the window at...Eggs had no idea what he was looking at.

It appeared to be a massive dish of strawberry ice cream in a colossal white ceramic bowl, but strawberry ice cream did not usually shriek. And this one was shrieking up a storm.

"*Aghhhhhhhhhhh!*" howled the ice cream as it began to quiver and flick off gobs of frothy whipped-cream stuff.

"It's a big Cheese Bit!" Eggs hissed.

Fish stood up and neatly tossed Eggs to the grass. They both Emergency Boxed themselves.

"Something was looking in my window!" the Cheese Bit in the ceramic bowl shrieked. "Something hideous was spying on me in the bath! A lady is no longer safe in her own boudoir!"

Because Eggs was really too large to fit entirely in his box, his head was sticking out. He caught sight of something in the driveway.

If that's what I think it is, we could really use one!
Eggs thought. He crept toward it. He was right—it was
a wheelbarrow!

"Guys, over here!" Eggs whispered.

Wheels got there first. He lifted the wheelbarrow's
handles, kicked the tire, and gave a wild gurgle of
approval. Fish gave the signal for them to retreat with
their prize and make for the nearest manhole.

As they raced down the street, Eggs could hardly
contain his own pride. His first junky-bit! And it wasn't
just any junky-bit—it was a wheelbarrow! It was a find-
sie even the most grizzled and experienced Boxtroll
would have been proud of!

"There's the manhole," Eggs called, urging them
on. Shoe was in the lead, Fish was making sure Eggs
kept up in the middle, and Wheels was moving a little
slower, bringing up the rear. A loud, sudden *whump*
brought them up short. Fish shoved Eggs toward an old
barrel and Eggs dove into it. For a moment, Eggs heard
nothing at all. Very cautiously, making sure his eye-
beams were switched off, he peeked over the top of the
barrel.

At first, he did not realize what he was seeing.
Wheels was there, lying down in the street, struggling

like he was trying to remove a heavy blanket. *Maybe I can get that thing off him,* Eggs thought, standing up so he could climb out of the barrel. Then he heard footsteps, and he dropped to the bottom of the barrel in a crouch. Outside, he heard a familiar voice.

"Gentlemen! Do you smell what I smell?"

It's the voice of the terrible red-hatted Cheese Bit, Eggs thought. *The one called Snatcher. The one with a truck that says "Boxtroll Exterminator."*

"Oh, no," whispered Eggs. "Poor Wheels!"

Very carefully, Eggs peered over the top of the barrel. He pressed his hand over his mouth to cover his groan of dismay. Eggs had seen these Cheese Bits before—they were burned into his memory.

A huge, menacing silhouette of a man wearing an enormous stovepipe hat loomed into view. Snatcher! And in the street, climbing out of the boxy red vehicle, were the other three Red Hats Eggs had seen the day he peeked Aboveground.

"Smell?" asked the gangly, tall Red Hat.

"You heard me, Mr. Pickles," Snatcher snapped. "That, my friends, is the rotten stench of fear. As you can see, Mr. Gristle has already captured one of them with the net gun. Mr. Trout, take care of it."

Eggs gripped the sides of the barrel, his eyes huge. He didn't want to watch. He didn't want to see any of this. But he couldn't look away.

The boulder-sized Red Hat called Trout bent over the squirming and struggling Wheels, who was still trapped in the net, and lifted him, net and all, in his arms.

"Into the truck with it," Pickles cried, doing some kind of victory dance by springing from one long, skinny leg to the other. "Another villain off the streets. And where's our reward?"

"The reward of a thing well done," Trout recited, tossing Wheels into the truck and slamming the door, "is having done it."

Pickles's face fell.

"I meant, like, a big trophy," Pickles said. "Don't you think, Gristle?"

"Quiet, I'm trying to smell the fear," barked the waddling Gristle. "Fear," he repeated in a low, villainous voice.

Eggs dropped lower in the barrel as Pickles and Gristle began rooting through a pile of old boxes on the street. Of Snatcher's three Red Hat minions, Eggs got the idea that Gristle—with his dead eyes and his permanent sneering snarl—was definitely the scariest.

They're searching for more of us, Eggs thought in horror. His heart began to hammer in his chest. Was he going to be captured his very first night hunting? Fish would be beside himself with worry!

"You ever smell fear, Mr. Trout?" asked Pickles.

"I believe the boss was speaking symbolical, Mr. Pickles," said Trout, glancing nervously at Snatcher before kicking an empty box to one side.

"Me, I smelled a ferret once. Big fella, too. Stuck in me chimney, he was," Pickles declared.

"No, no, it was a *metaphor.* You can't smell a metaphor. You know, like how Macbeth called fear a dagger of the mind, a fa—"

"Thassright, that ferret screamed all night," Pickles interrupted. "So I spoze I *heard* fear. But nope, I never smelled it."

"Crimminy, didn't you hear what I said? You're as dumb as one of these boxes, Pickles, you really are," Trout muttered as he kicked another box, which flew in the air and landed at Pickles's feet. A squeak erupted from inside.

Oh, no, Eggs thought. *Don't let them have found someone else.*

"Got one!" Pickles yelled, pulling out a squirming Boxtroll.

Eggs put his hand over his eyes. He couldn't bear to see who it was. It was all just too awful.

"Come on, ya squirmy monster. Your days of evil-doing have just come to an end," Pickles's voice continued.

"What, you really think Boxtrolls understand the duality of good and evil?" Trout asked.

Eggs heard the truck door open, then slam.

"They must, right? I mean, why else would they hide from us? We *are* the good guys."

"No, you aren't," muttered Eggs. "Cheese Bits are monsters."

"Yeah, I suppose we are the good guys," Trout said. "Find any more?"

Eggs heard the sound of another box being kicked. He winced.

"There! *There!*" Snatcher bellowed. "Two more! Quickly, Mr. Gristle. *Acquire them!*"

Two more? Eggs decided to take a chance and peek out of the barrel again.

His stomach lurched. It was Fish and Shoe. And

they realized they'd been seen. As Eggs watched helplessly, the two Boxtrolls made a break for it, dashing across the street and vaulting over a fence that led to a small alley.

"*Acquire!*" bellowed Gristle, following them across the street. "I'm gonna smash them with my bat!"

The alley fence did not slow Gristle down. He simply ran right through it, bits of wood and hinges raining down onto the cobblestones. In his barrel, Eggs dropped into a crouch in a terrified, shaking ball, with his arms over his head. What would happen if they got Fish? How could Eggs survive without him?

"*Boom!*" yelled Gristle, swinging his bat wildly. Eggs flinched as he heard it connect with wood and brick.

"Wah? Where'd they go?" Gristle bellowed. "*Acquire!*"

Eggs heard heavy footsteps stampeding down the alley. After a moment, Pickles and Trout scampered after him.

"Follow Gristle, you two idiots," muttered Snatcher. More footsteps. Then Eggs heard the sound of an engine being started. Snatcher was driving away.

Slowly, Eggs tried to stand up. His legs were shaking so badly, he had to grab the sides of the barrel to pull himself to his feet.

The street was empty.

Cautiously, still feeling as if he might be sick, Eggs emerged from the barrel. He crossed the street and peered down the alley. There was nothing there but an old, broken street cart.

But what do I do? Where do I go? Eggs wondered, biting his lip to stop himself from crying. He took a few shaky steps toward the street he thought might lead to a manhole. To his utter alarm, the old street cart began to follow him. Eggs froze in his tracks. Was this a Red Hat trick to bait and capture him?

The street cart tilted one way, then the other, then toppled to the ground with a crash. Two large pieces of it seemed to suddenly grow arms, legs, and heads.

"Fish! Shoe!" Eggs cried, almost hysterical with relief. He rushed toward his friends, then looked up and down the street.

"They got Wheels, they got Wheels!" Eggs whispered. "And I think they got someone else, too, but I didn't see who." Even as he said it, Eggs found it hard to believe. Red Hats had snatched Wheels right in front of his eyes. For the first time, Eggs fully understood the horror facing the Boxtrolls. The danger that faced them every night when they hunted, and diminished their numbers slowly and steadily.

Until what? Eggs thought miserably. *Until every last one of us is gone?*

Fish gave Eggs a little shake, to snap him out of his fear. He firmly gripped Eggs's hand, and the three of them raced across the street and down the sidewalk. The wheelbarrow was still there, lying on its side next to the manhole cover. Shoe yanked open the manhole, and before Eggs could protest that the wheelbarrow should go first, Fish gave him a shove.

For months, Eggs had imagined what it would feel like to whiz down the series of tunnels and drop through the chute onto the conveyor belt. But now Eggs barely noticed or cared. Everything was a blur until he shot out of the chute spout, bumped down the conveyor belt, and landed on the big pillow on the cavern floor.

Eggs stood up, adjusted his box, and let his eyes adapt to the light. Usually, the sight of the cavern was the most beautiful thing in the world to him—he could never get enough of the mass of workshops and inter-connected machines: the waterwheel fashioned from junky-bits, the giant chandelier sun of hundreds of old bulbs wired together, and the constellation of lights and symphony of sounds that flickered and buzzed like an amusement park. But now he felt nothing; he was numb.

Something on the belt was making a clattering noise, and the wheelbarrow came flying off and landed upside down. Fish came zooming down behind it, followed by Shoe.

Fish picked up the wheelbarrow and set it on its side. He gave the wheel a spin with his claw and nodded. Shoe quietly smacked his box, then smacked Eggs's box, too.

"That's it?" Eggs asked. "We just go on like nothing happened?"

Shoe made an unintelligible noise and walked away, pushing the wheelbarrow.

Fish hesitated, looking deep into Eggs's eyes. Eggs had never seen such enormous sadness on his friend's face. Eggs looked down, embarrassed. Of course they were not acting as if nothing happened. They would each grieve in their own way, but not while there was work to be done in the cavern. And always it seemed there was more work than they could handle.

"I know," Eggs said. "That wheelbarrow could fix the problem with the waterwheel. Work has to go on. I've never seen this many bulbs dark in our sun. I remember when I couldn't look straight at it without seeing spots. And when did the clock stop chiming? Fish, things are breaking faster than we can find junky-bits to fix them. And now I think I know why. There aren't many Boxtrolls left."

Fish stared at Eggs with unblinking lemon eyes. The sadness had left his face. Now Fish simply looked determined.

"Things aren't ever going to be the same, are they?" Eggs asked. "The Red Hats have taken too many of us. This is it, right? Just tell me, Fish. I just want to know. The end is nigh, isn't it? This is the Boxtroll apocalypse."

Fish gave Eggs a short, excruciatingly tight hug, his claws making a *scrabbity-scrabble* sound as they scraped over Eggs's box. Then he waddled away to catch up with Shoe.

"Fine, then," Eggs said as loudly as he could. "I'll just go to my nook and work on my Music Machine. Play a tune, maybe." *Not that there is going to be any dancing tonight,* Eggs thought glumly.

Eggs sighed, then headed for the carousel troll-lift chairs. He had to let several go by before he found one with an unbroken seat. The troll-lift squeaked and shuddered and *clickety-clack*ed its way up the cavern wall. Eggs steadied himself, then jumped off onto a familiar ledge carved into the rock, its surface smooth and shiny from centuries of Boxtroll feet.

A little Quattro Sabatinos would be comforting, Eggs said to himself. *I still say this is the best album they ever put out.*

The cardboard cover to the old record had faded and suffered from the handling of too many Boxtroll claws, but the color photograph of the Sabatinos in question was still visible. Eggs stared at it as he had so often before, regarding the four creatures who resembled Cheese Bits only in their general size and coloring. Eggs usually could never get enough of the elaborate swirl of fur each Sabatino had under his nose, of their magnificent striped outer garments where a box would normally be worn, of the marvelous vanilla-colored, flattish discs they each wore on their heads, in the same way the Cheese Bits wore their red hats.

Eggs slid the flat vinyl disc from the cardboard cover and placed it carefully on his Music Machine's turntable. When he flicked the switch to the On position, the turntable began making a high-pitched squeak with each rotation.

"Darn it, that won't do," Eggs muttered.

He turned so he was facing the cavern, and shouted, "Hey, Oil Can? Can you—?"

Eggs's voice faded. He remembered that Oil Can had been gone a long time. And now there was no Wheels, either. And he still didn't know who else the Red Hats had captured tonight. He didn't want to know.

Eggs sat on the ground, pulled his knees to his chest, and very quietly began to cry.

Chapter 3

Winnie placed a pair of cheddar-orange earmuffs on her head and pressed down tight.

It was no good. She could still hear the bellowing, thunderous voices of her father and his guests downstairs. The Tasting Room had a strong, stout wooden door, and Winnie's bedroom was clear at the other end of the Cheese Guild—one of the largest and grandest buildings in all of Cheesebridge. But it made no difference. They could probably be heard in outer space once they started going on about cheese. It's all they ever seemed to want to discuss. Cheese, cheese, cheese.

"Ugh. It's so grating," Winnie muttered, throwing the earmuffs down in disgust.

Looks like it's another night holed up in my room alone, she thought ruefully. *I'm the most miserable girl in Cheesebridge.*

She flopped down on her soft bed, smacking away the ruffle-edged pillows that covered it. Lying on her stomach, propped up on her elbows, Winnie leafed through the latest issue of *Citizen Cheesebridge* magazine.

There was a gory article with pictures about the Trubshaw baby. They ran the same thing every year before the anniversary, but Winnie couldn't help scanning the illustrations of the crime scene and reading the lurid interviews with experts offering theories as to exactly what had happened to that baby.

A shudder rippled up Winnie's spine.

"Pure evil. You'd have to be, to boil a baby alive," Winnie murmured, feeling her arms erupt in goose bumps. "And only Pure Evil would have the stomach to eat someone's eyeballs and make soup of their innards."

Winnie turned the page. LOCAL EXPERTS SAY NO ONE IS SAFE, read the headline. The expert, someone named Mr. A. Res-Natch, had a very convincing theory that the abduction and gruesome murder of the Trubshaw baby had been simply a test run to begin a long-term study of the highly efficient Red Hat protection team. He said the fiendish monsters known as Boxtrolls were now ready to unleash a secret weapon to battle the Red Hats while the Boxtrolls went after the citizens of

Cheesebridge. Res-Natch noted that children of all ages were especially vulnerable. Winnie began reading out loud.

> RES-NATCH TOLD THIS REPORTER, "NO ONE IS SAFE. THERE ARE MONSTERS OUT THERE, AND THEY WANT TO CHEW YOUR LIMBS OFF AND ROAST YOUR SKULL IN A CAULDRON AND BAKE YOUR FINGERS IN LIGHTLY SALTED CORNMEAL BREADING. SO FAR, THE VALIANT EFFORTS OF ARCHIBALD SNATCHER AND HIS CRACK TEAM OF RED HATS HAVE KEPT CHEESEBRIDGE SAFE. BUT AN EVIL PLOT IS UNFOLDING. THE TIME WILL BE SOON, AND THE STREETS WILL RUN WITH BLOOD."

Winnie pressed her hand to her heart. "My word!" she exclaimed. Then she continued to read.

> WHEN THIS REPORTER PRESSED RES-NATCH TO GIVE A MORE SPECIFIC IDEA OF WHEN THE BLOODBATH WOULD RESUME, HIS ONLY RESPONSE WAS TO ASK, "WHAT IS THE BLOODIEST, MOST SOMBER, MOST GRUESOME DAY OF THE YEAR?"

Trubshaw Baby Day, of course. Tomorrow.

Winnie pushed the magazine under a blanket and lay back on the pillows, her eyes wide.

Maybe Res-Natch is right, Winnie thought. Maybe the Boxtroll monsters were just getting started with the Trubshaw baby. Maybe they really had been building a secret weapon all this time, so they could start feasting on Cheesebridgians again.

Maybe, Winnie told herself, *they are already here.*

Suddenly, Winnie sat bolt upright in bed, clutching her hands to the neck of her nightgown.

At the window just by her bed—*outside* the window, to be precise—something had moved. Winnie was sure of it. She sat frozen, staring straight ahead, afraid to budge. It was after dark, well after curfew. Anyone in Cheesebridge who had any business going anywhere was already downstairs in the Tasting Room with her father.

*Could it have been one of the...*Winnie dared not even finish the thought. Moving with greatly exaggerated casualness, she stretched and pretended to struggle through a galaxy-sized yawn. Slowly, arms still overhead in a boy-I'm-just-tuckered-out stretch, she maneuvered herself closer to the window. When she could take the suspense no longer, she dropped her arms and pressed her face right up against the glass.

"Monsters!" Winnie shrieked at the top of her lungs. Then she smacked her hand over her mouth to stifle her gasp. She dove face-first back onto the bed and pulled a pillow over her head.

Could Mr. A. Res-Natch have hit the nail on the head? Were they ready for this? Like all children, Winnie had to participate in occasional after-school Boxtroll Buster programs, learning what to look for outside your window in the morning to see if they'd been watching you, what sorts of sounds to listen for, the importance of observing the strict curfew laws. But for all her careful attention, Winnie had only thought one, maybe two times before that she might have glimpsed a bit of something, a strange whatsit, gone in the blink of an eye, that might possibly have been monster related. But she had never heard a sound right under her window. She had never seen a shadow that had never been there before. And they did say in Boxtroll Busters that the monsters liked to cluster under windows at night and spy on their prey.

Maybe just one more little peek.

Winnie got up and pressed her face to the glass again. She scanned Market Square below, which was covered in a layer of heavy fog. For a moment, the moon emerged from behind a cloud, shining directly through the fog.

"Maybe I've been cooped up in here too long," Winnie muttered. "I guess my eyes were just playing tricks on me. There's nothing there but a couple of old boxes."

Then Winnie gasped and drew back. The boxes seemed to shift and change position, but that was not what startled her. What she saw was a beam of moonlight highlighting something coming out of one of the boxes, a pale, ghostly face the color of Swiss cheese, with large eyes that seemed to be looking right at her and a mouth that dropped into an O when it saw her looking right back.

"It *is* monsters!" Winnie cried, reaching up and yanking the curtains shut. Oh, why, why had she taken that second look?

"They might have seen me," she whispered. "They could be coming for me right now! They could be on their way to the Cheese Guild to catch me and eat my eyeballs! I'd best warn Father."

Winnie leapt off the bed and grabbed her bathrobe, still giddy from the shock and trying very hard to feel the complete and utter terror of a girl who was very likely about to be torn limb from limb and consumed alive in small, fanged bites.

"My goodness, this is so *exciting!*" Winnie said, throwing open her bedroom door and racing through the hallway and down the wide set of stairs.

The sound of voices and laughter grew much louder as Winnie scampered toward a heavy set of double wooden doors marked by an enormous brass plate engraved with the words WHITE HAT MEMBERS ONLY.

Winnie pounded on the door as hard as she could. She knew Father would be vexed if she entered the Tasting Room without permission, especially during one of his meetings. But the voices kept right on inside as if they hadn't heard her. Winnie heard her father's voice temporarily rise above the others.

"Settle down, men, settle down. Important town business to discuss, yes? First on the docket, we have more complaints about crumbling bridges."

A braying voice interrupted.

"Speaking of crumbling...is that a new blue cheese I see there, Lord Portley-Rind?"

A chorus of voices jumbled one over another.

"Does smell delicious..."

"Oh, I say, a bit of the old blue *would* liven things up...."

"Now that you mention it, it *is* rather hard to concentrate with it sitting right there in plain view, really...."

Winnie knocked again, this time so hard her knuckles ached, but the voices just babbled more loudly about "blue" and "ripe" and "just a taste." Taking a deep breath, she turned the knob and pushed the door open.

The Tasting Room was a dark, luxuriously furnished rotunda, its walls lined with cases upon cases of cheeses. Winnie wrinkled her nose. She had never liked this room, even when it stood empty in the cold light of day. It was like a smelly Victorian man cave. At the moment, much of the smell was emanating from a table in the center of the room, on which had been laid out an alarming assortment of cheeses of all shapes and sizes, some gooey and oozing, some speckled and angry, some covered in bright red rinds that made them look embarrassed to be caught out.

Around the table sat four finely dressed gentlemen, each wearing a spotless white stovepipe hat. They were all staring very hard at a wedge of blue cheese sitting just in front of Winnie's father.

"Well," Lord Portley-Rind said, "I suppose we *could* do with a bit of a nibble first."

At that, all the men fell upon the cheeses like a pack of exceptionally well-mannered jackals. Winnie wrinkled her nose at the sight. Each man oohed and aahed over each bite, taking great pains to examine and sniff the cheese before popping it into his mouth with gusto.

"Mmmm, remarkable," Winnie's father proclaimed. "It's pungent...coarse...a bit veiny....But enough about your wife, Boulanger!"

There was a chorus of *mwahaha*s and *hear hear*s as the men clapped one another on the back. Horrified, Winnie snuck a look at Lord Boulanger, but the old geezer seemed to be laughing as hard as the rest of the White Hats.

"It's true!" wheezed Boulanger, sitting up straight in his wheelchair and holding up a quivering glob of gooey something or other, then triumphantly popping it into his mouth.

"Excuse me?" Winnie called, but she might as well have been addressing a brick of cheddar. Her father had still not even registered her presence. He stood up abruptly and began reading from a piece of paper. A small glob of blue cheese dangled from one corner of it.

"All good fun, gentlemen, but we do have this school funding initiative to vote on this evening. Been sitting here for months, or so I'm told. Now…"

Winnie's father paused to take a breath and took advantage of the opportunity to insert another slice of something into his mouth.

"Mmm!" he exclaimed, his eyebrows shooting up. "Surprisingly sharp!"

The White Hats seized the opportunity to taste the cheese that had so enlivened Lord Portley-Rind.

"Complex," mused one of the men, another crony of her father's. *Langsdale*, Winnie thought. *That's his name.* When they were eating, it was sometimes hard to tell them apart.

"I'm tasting an underflavor of…plum," said Lord Boulanger with his mouth mostly full.

Gross. Winnie averted her eyes. It was enough to put a girl off cheese for life.

Winnie's father waved his hands around, trying to regain control of the meeting. He cleared his throat.

"Now, all in favor of, uh…all in favor of…" Lord Portley-Rind's voice trailed off as he knitted his brows and concentrated on remembering exactly what they were supposed to be working on.

"Of cutting open the Roquefort next!" shouted Sir Broderick, the youngest and perhaps most gluttonous of the group.

"Aye!" they all shouted in unison. Lord Boulanger shouted so loudly, his hat listed to one side.

"Okay, okay," Lord Portley-Rind conceded, with little or no reluctance. "But a quick reminder, gentlemen, that tomorrow is Trubshaw Baby Day. And we all know what that means...."

To Winnie's complete and soul-rattling horror, her father began making kissing noises and blinking his eyes coquettishly.

"That's right," he continued, his lips still grotesquely pursed, "it means a performance by Madame Frou Frou!"

There was a chorus of falsetto *oo-la-la*s, and a burst of steam shot out of the little engine on Lord Boulanger's wheelchair.

"*A vision!*" the old man shouted enthusiastically.

"Now, there's a woman with some cheese on her bones," Sir Broderick agreed heartily.

Lord Portley-Rind half closed his eyes, held a fat piece of Brie in the air, and proclaimed, "A lady like Frou Frou resembles a fine piece of Brie. The soft, smooth exterior, and inside—oh, the melty, milky—"

Winnie could not prevent a squeak of disgust from escaping her mouth. This time, her father *did* notice her, and stopped midsentence, to Winnie's extreme relief.

"*Winifred!*" he bellowed in outrage, clutching the Brie so hard it exploded, the insides shooting out like a stream of gelatinous lava. A large blob landed directly on his hat, and his face reddened with anger. He stormed toward his daughter.

"It is *long* past your bedtime," he thundered, gesturing toward the door.

"I *was* in bed," Winnie protested. "But I saw something outside. Through the window. You must *all* listen to me." She paused for a moment, to build up the dramatic effect a little. Then, as loudly, clearly, and importantly as she could, she made her announcement.

"I saw the Boxtrolls again!!!"

Chapter 4

The response was...well, there wasn't one.

Lord Portley-Rind had already halfway forgotten about his daughter, distracted as he was by the sight of his peers tucking into another of his prized cheeses.

"That's nice, dear," he mumbled, licking his lips.

Winnie stomped her foot in frustration. Why must he always be this way? Why would he never listen to her? All he cared about was his precious cheese!

"It's *not* nice!" Winnie yelled. "Listen to me! I saw them, and they were *right* outside, and they could be coming to rip the flesh off my bones and eat my eyeballs right this very minute!"

No one was even looking at her. Her father's three companions were muttering and exclaiming to one another, but not about Boxtrolls.

"Mmmm, quite the curd," said Lord Boulanger.

"Would be a shame to miss this one, Portley-Rind," added Sir Broderick.

"Tuck in, won't you, old boy," urged Langsdale.

Winnie thought if her father stared at that cheese any harder, his eyes were going to explode right out of his head.

"Yes, yes, just one moment, gentlemen! Leave some for me!" he pleaded. "Now, Winifred, really. A proper girl should not be obsessing over grotesque monsters. It's quite unseemly."

He's really one to talk, Winnie thought. *He still has a blob of cheese hanging off of his hat.*

"I'm *not* obsessed," she argued. "But they're practically inside the Cheese Guild, and I can't stop imagining them gnawing off my toes and stringing them together as a necklace. They do that, you know!"

Her father's eyes were still fixed on the cheese. A droplet of saliva glimmered in the corner of his mouth.

"Mmm-hmmm. That's good, my dear," he murmured, as if in a daze. He patted Winnie on the top of her head.

Winnie narrowed her eyes.

"Father, tell me something. If the Boxtrolls kidnapped me right now and slurped up my intestines like noodles—because they do that, you know—would you give up your white hat if it was the only way to save me?"

"Yes, dear," her father mumbled.

Winnie exhaled with frustration.

"You aren't listening to *a word I say!*" she hollered as loud as she could.

Her father blinked at her a few times, as if he had just partially awakened from a long bout of sleepwalking.

"Whuh? Uh…a word.…You said 'white hat.' White hat!"

Lord Portley-Rind's hand automatically flew up to lovingly touch his own white hat. He looked dismayed when his fingers encountered the blob of cheese.

"Oh, my. It seems to have been smudged by a bit of Brie. Be a dear, Winifred, and have the butler give this a wash, would you?"

He passed the hat to Winnie with one hand while firmly pushing her out the door with the other. Winnie was practically speechless.

"But…but…" she began.

The door slammed shut in her face.

Now that *was really cold, even for Father,* Winnie thought, her disbelief slowly turning to anger. She could hear his voice happily blabbering away through the door.

"Back to important White Hat business," he declared, to a general wheezy cheer. "Pass the Camembert!"

Winnie shook her head in disgust, backing away from the door and clutching his precious white hat a little too hard.

"'Important White Hat business,'" she mimicked, rolling her eyes. "More like dumb...old man...disgusting cheese business!"

She stormed up the stairs and back to her room and slammed the door loudly, not that anyone would hear it, or care if they did.

In her room, Winnie stood, fuming.

I am so *tired,* she thought, *of taking a backseat to* cheese. *Nothing is* ever *going to change in this house. Father will never look twice at me unless I turn into a piece of cheese myself.*

Winnie clutched the white hat even tighter. Her eye fell on the set of double doors that led to a small balcony off her room. She marched over, flung the doors open, and stomped out onto the balcony, barely noticing the chill of the night air.

"I'll take care of your precious white hat for you," she muttered. "Here, how's *this*?"

With that, Winnie flung the hat up and out as hard as she could. It sailed into the night like a disk-shaped toy, glowing eerily in the moonlight as it descended slowly, then skittered to a stop on the far side of Market Square.

"There," Winnie declared with satisfaction, brushing her hands together and complimenting herself on a job well done. As she stared at the place where the hat had landed, the smile faded from her face.

Next to cheese, there was nothing in the world her father and his cronies cared about more than those stupid white hats. Most everyone in Cheesebridge knew that whatever you did, and whoever you did it to, you'd best not tinker with the white hat of a White Hat.

"Okaaaay, that may not have been the brightest thing I ever did," Winnie said. "Darn it!"

She raced back inside, making for the main staircase. Monsters or not, she had to run out there and get the stupid hat back. She could only hope it hadn't landed in something unfortunate, like a steaming pile of horse droppings.

At the excessively fortified front door, Winnie began unbolting the locks as the sound of giddy, cheese-drunk laughter echoed from the Tasting Room. Gingerly,

Winnie opened the door just a crack and peered outside. The vast, empty Market Square was punctuated by the occasional small circle of lamplight. The rest lay in moonshadow, looking like an enormous lake of black ice. It was absolutely silent. At the far end of the square, a single ray of moonlight illuminated the white hat, as if she was being dared to retrieve it.

Winnie gulped and took one step forward. She was now technically outside, though her hand still rested on the doorknob.

I have to stop breathing so loud, she thought. She held her breath for a moment and listened, straining to hear anything that might indicate something menacing lurking in the shadows. Somewhere off to the right she heard something make a rustling sound, like *shabasha-bashaba.* Was that one of them?

You can do this, she told herself. And what was the worst that could happen? She could be torn into squishy bits by monster claws and leave no trace for the authorities, save for a few bloody shreds of nightgown.

But that would be better than facing Father when he finds out I threw his hat into the street, Winnie thought.

Steeling herself, Winnie crept down the stairs and cautiously slunk forward, as quietly and carefully as a cat. She had only taken a few steps when she heard a sharp sound, like a fork tapping another fork, *doink doink doink*. She stopped, every muscle in her body tensing. She squinted hard in the direction of the sound.

"I think there's something there," whispered Winnie. "I really, actually, totally think there is something right...over...there...."

She took a deep, shaky breath, then darted forward again, faster this time, and made a little more noise. And she heard the sound again, and froze.

What the heck is that?

It sounded like the skittering of leaves over a crust of snow.

Or the sound of claws on cobblestones.

There was now no doubt in Winnie's mind. The Boxtrolls were stalking her. And judging by the different directions the sounds had come from, there were lots of them: hundreds, maybe thousands! And they had her surrounded.

Winnie took off again, this time at a dead run. But the skittering sound followed her. And it was louder now.

She spun around in a full circle but saw nothing.

Of course I don't see anything, Winnie thought. *They always say in* Boxtroll Busters *that the monsters can disappear right in front of you.*

Or reappear right behind you. Winnie suddenly knew without a sliver of doubt that someone—something—was standing behind her. She could feel it watching her, invisible twin rays boring into her back.

"I'm gonna die," she whispered.

Even as she said it, she caught a glimpse of the hat on the cobblestones a short way off and realized she'd gotten quite close. Maybe if she *did* die, and they found her remains clutching the precious white hat, maybe then she would be remembered kindly. Perhaps her father would even have a small statue built. Or create an entire day for mourning her, as he had for the poor Trubshaw baby! Maybe next year, Mr. A. Res-Natch would give an interview about Winifred Portley-Rind, mercilessly slaughtered in the flower of her youth by the Trubshaw baby's ravenous, blood-craving abductors.

Gentlemen were supposed to die with their boots on. Winnie felt it only proper that she die with a hat on. The white hat.

She moved forward, beginning to reach out. There was another echo of a scuttle, and then the mist lifted and a hunched silhouette with glowing eyes came into view.

"Who's there?" Winnie cried.

Oh, that was stupid! What two things were most often people's last words in horror stories? "Hello?" and "Who's there?" Winnie might as well have signed her own death warrant.

She managed one terrified squeak before pressing her hands over her mouth. Not that it mattered. The... thing had seen her. It was coming closer.

Winnie closed her eyes tight and prepared to spill her young, noble blood all over the cobblestones of Market Square. They would find her body at first light—a watchman would come grim-faced to the Cheese Guild door....The shrieks and wails of her devastated mother would set mothers all over town springing out of bed and clutching their children close to them. Word would begin to spread, and the streets would fill with the sobbing of women and the raging of men, the same desperate words uttered again and again...:"No, not Winifred, not Winifred Portley-Rind!

That young, exquisite angel of a child murdered and eaten by Boxtrolls? *No!*"

A fat tear rolled down Winnie's cheek. It really was very tragic.

After a few moments, when she was not dead yet, Winnie opened her eyes.

It was standing right in front of her.

But now that she could see it better, Winnie realized what she had taken for huge glowing eyes were actually two small lights fixed to either side of a pair of old goggles. And what she had taken for the shape of a Boxtroll was actually just an old box being worn as some sort of...fashion statement, maybe. She tilted her head to one side. Why, this wasn't a Boxtroll at all!

"Who are you, boy?" she asked.

The boy lifted the goggles from his face and stared at her with perplexed brown eyes.

"I don't think I know you. Do you live here in Cheesebridge, boy?"

Winnie's question seemed to have stupefied him. His mouth was working furiously, but no words were coming out of it.

What a strange child, Winnie thought. *Why is he wandering around after dark all alone, wearing those strange goggles and a dirty cardboard shirt with a picture of an egg on it?*

There was a sudden burst of skittering noises. Winnie shrieked and jumped back as something grabbed the boy's shoulder and she saw the glint of something yellow and jewel shaped in the dark. The boy shot one look at Winnie over his shoulder, then disappeared into the shadows.

Taken! Taken by a Boxtroll!

Winnie could hardly believe what she had just seen. Were they not going to kill him right there? Maybe it was true....People said the Trubshaw baby had been dragged down to a Death Cave to be murdered.

"Hey, come back!" Winnie called.

It was a bad move, Winnie instantly realized.

I seem to be having some issues with impulse control tonight, Winnie thought.

A car horn blared and Winnie shrieked, nearly jumping out of her skin. Twin columns of headlights suddenly sliced through the night, illuminating sections of Market Square. It must be Red Hats out hunting Boxtrolls—no one else would dare drive after curfew. Thank heavens for the Red Hats! Maybe they would get to the boy in time.

Winnie watched as the vehicle seemed to idle. Then it careered forward and banked to the left. All at once the headlights illuminated three figures at the corner of the square. It was the boy and, standing in front of him defensively, the Boxtrolls who had snatched him!

Maybe the Red Hats can still get him, Winnie thought. *Poor boy. He must be awfully poor to be living on the street with nothing to wear but an old bit of cardboard.*

Why didn't I offer him money or something? Winnie chided herself. *Although the Boxtrolls probably would have just eaten it along with the rest of him.*

The Red Hat truck's horn blared again, and the Boxtrolls took off with their captive, though, oddly, it seemed to Winnie as if the boy was actually running *with* the Boxtrolls, even appearing to help one when it stumbled. The truck raced after them, disappearing around the corner. Now the square was dark and quiet again. What a night! No one was going to believe that she had witnessed a Boxtroll abduction. She, Winifred Portley-Rind, had seen it all happen, had looked death right in the face. She, Winifred Portley-Rind, had gotten closer to Boxtrolls than any human being except the Red Hats and had lived to tell the tale, lived to bear witness to their powers of camouflage, their stealth, and their strange yellow eyes.

I did think they'd be taller, Winnie thought.

It hadn't really hit her yet. And of course not—she had just survived a close encounter of the troll kind. She was in shock. That's what happened to people who had terrifying brushes with death. They went into shock, and you put a blanket on them.

That's what I need, Winnie told herself. *A blanket. Then I can really begin to process the horror.*

She just had to grab her father's hat and run like crazy for the Cheese Guild. But before she could take a step, a dark shadow loomed over her, a towering ghostly shape that seemed to hiss with malevolence, the white hat clutched tightly in one of its hideous hands.

Chapter 5

M y, my, someone is out past curfew!" said the thing. "Very dangerous, my child. Why, I do believe it's young Winifred Portley-Rind!"

Winnie took a step backward and stared into the cold, glittering eyes of Archibald Snatcher.

"Well, I saw a—" Winnie began.

"A what?" Snatcher said, leaning forward eagerly.

He really was repulsive. His skin had an unhealthy grayish sheen, and his jowls quivered like jelly under his oversized fish mouth. It was all Winnie could do not to wrinkle her nose and say "Yuck." Red Hat or not, something epic had just happened to Winnie. And no one in the world knew it yet. Winnie didn't want creepy, horrid Mr. Snatcher to pepper her with questions. She didn't want to spend another minute in his company.

"Just a boy," Winnie said. "A lost boy."

"Really?" sneered Snatcher. "All I saw were a couple of filthy Boxtroll monsters."

He surveyed Winnie with a slick, oily smile that made her feel sick to her stomach.

"Well, Miss Portley-Rind, do allow me to escort you safely home to your esteemed father."

Ew.

"No thank you," Winnie replied hastily. "I can escort myself. If you'll just give me my father's hat back, I'll be on my way."

Snatcher tucked the hat under one arm and began striding toward the Guild. Winnie had to scramble to keep up. This was an escort?

"Mmm, yes, how did this hat find itself aaaall the way out here, I wonder?" Snatcher said, smiling unpleasantly.

"It was…well, actually, the wind blew it. Right out the window," Winnie said, making an unsuccessful grab for the hat.

Snatcher licked his revolting finger and held it up in the air.

"Wind, you say? How peculiar. Seems to have died away completely," he said as they reached the front steps of the Cheese Guild.

"Most peculiar, indeed," Winnie said, mimicking Snatcher's fake-friendly tone as she made another lunge for the hat. He deftly moved the hat out of her reach.

"Well, I do thank you for the escort, Mr. Snatcher," Winnie said. "And here we are, safely back at the Cheese Guild. There's no need to go inside."

Winnie held her hand out for the hat, and Snatcher practically smacked it away.

"Oh, as a gentleman, I must *insist!*" he brayed, climbing the stairs and opening the front door.

"Hey! You can't just—"

But the reptilian Snatcher had already slithered inside. Sputtering with anger, Winnie chased after him.

"Helllooooooooo? Lord Portley-Rind?" Snatcher called in a mincing falsetto voice.

I should have seen it coming, she thought. *Snatcher is the biggest suck-up in all of Cheesebridge. Of course he's not going to let a chance to ingratiate himself with Father get away, even it means getting me in huge trouble.*

Winnie raced into the front hall behind him.

"Will you *please* just give me back the hat now?" she pleaded.

Snatcher turned and gave her an especially ugly smile. He looked like a hideous old lizard in an over-sized red hat. He whisked her father's hat behind his back and made a beeline for the main staircase. Winnie chased after him. They were halfway up when she made another grab for the hat, but Snatcher just danced around her. At the same moment, to Winnie's dismay, the door to the Tasting Room flew open and her father emerged.

"What in heaven is going on out here?" he demanded. Then he caught sight of Snatcher on the staircase, and his mouth dropped open.

"Archibald Snatcher? Am I suffering hallucinations from an overextended strain of cheese mold? What in the world are you doing here?"

Snatcher managed to spin around and bow deeply at the same time. Unfortunately for Winnie, he pulled off both without losing his balance and falling down the stairs.

I should have given him a good shove, Winnie thought.

"My lord," said Snatcher, still doubled over in his ridiculous bow. "My deeeeepest apologies for the intrusion. But I happened to find something in the street, Your Lordship, that I believe belongs to you."

To Winnie's utter disgust, Snatcher held the white hat aloft like it was some sort of trophy he had won after years of dedicated work.

"My white hat!" exclaimed Lord Portley-Rind, looking absolutely scandalized. Snatcher was ceremoniously descending the staircase like a princess making her grand entrance to the ball, but Lord Portley-Rind thundered up the stairs to meet him, attempting to pluck the hat from Snatcher's hand.

"I'll take *that!*" Lord Portley-Rind snapped through gritted teeth, yanking at the hat, which Snatcher resolutely refused to relinquish.

"Most certainly...with absolute...pleasure," said Snatcher through equally gritted teeth, still clutching on to the hat.

Good grief, Winnie thought. *They're like a couple of rats battling it out over a hunk of cheese.*

"Now, Snatcher," growled Lord Portley-Rind, pulling on the hat with all his might, "one doesn't acquire a white hat simply by picking it up...off the...streeeeeeeeet!"

Winnie's father won the tug-of-war and went sprawling backward into the banister, hat in hand.

"A white hat must be earned!" he added self-righteously, brushing his jacket off and drawing himself up to his full height.

"Through civic duty!" shouted someone. Winnie

looked down to see that the remainder of the Cheese Guild had gathered at the foot of the stairs to observe.

"Quite right, or through governance," added Lord Boulanger, bouncing energetically in his wheelchair.

"Or by being rich," exclaimed Sir Broderick, looking around with wild-eyed self-importance.

Snatcher descended the stairs and presented himself to the Guild with a deep suck-up of a bow.

"Oh, don't I know it, esteemed sirs," Snatcher said, his voice oozing with his desire to curry favor. "And I will earn my white hat, too, when I have destroyed every last Boxtroll in Cheesebridge!"

As Lord Portley-Rind came down the stairs, Snatcher began ever so casually to inch toward the Tasting Room, craning his neck to get a glimpse inside.

"Yes, well," Lord Portley-Rind said, giving Snatcher a disapproving look, "even so, there will still be one pest left among us."

Snatcher stopped wiggling toward the Tasting Room and scowled.

"Now, then, Snatcher, how the devil did my hat get outside for you to so conveniently find in the first place?"

Snatcher smirked and pointed up at Winnie, who was still standing on the stairs.

"I was told by my young *friend* here that the wind had something to do with it," Snatcher explained. "As outlandishly unlikely as *that* may seem."

Now Winnie's father was scowling at her.

Ugh.

"I'm sorry, Father," she began, "but—"

"*Sorry!*" Snatcher interrupted, heading for the door. "Would love to stay, but must rush off—far too much work to do!"

He made a great show of tipping his red hat first to Lord Portley-Rind and then to Winnie.

"Miss Portley-Rind, Your Lordship, esteemed sirs…I'm sure we'll be seeing each other again very, very soon," Snatcher said as he oozed out the door like a giant slug.

Winnie's father barely gave the Red Hat a second glance. He was too busy glowering at his daughter.

"Winifred…" he began.

The front door flew open, and Snatcher reappeared like a persistent flea infestation.

"By the way, my hat size is six and a half! Never hurts to order ahead of time!" Snatcher sang.

Then he was gone before anyone could respond.

"Father, I was trying to say I'm really sorry! I didn't mean to do it—that is, well, I sort of did in the beginning, but I think you'll see that this situation actually offers a great opportunity for a father and daughter to discuss their feelings about things that—"

Lord Portley-Rind rolled his eyes and made a move toward the Tasting Room.

"*Wait!*" Winnie shouted. "Listen to me. I saw something out there! A boy! A strange boy I've never seen before, in a cardboard shirt, just standing out there with Boxtrolls, and—"

"*Not! Another! Word!*" Winnie's father ordered, one hand raised as though he were a traffic cop stopping cars.

"But, Father!"

"*Bed!*" Lord Portley-Rind hollered.

He swept into the tasting room, practically pursued by his three companions. The door slammed with a resounding *blam*.

Winnie stood alone, staring at the closed door.

"I did see a boy..." she said. "And it means something, and it ought to be investigated, and if Father can't see it, then he's got cheese-rot on the brain, that's all."

Shaking off her sadness and focusing on how right she was, and how everyone in Cheesebridge would see it one day and be sorry, Winnie wearily climbed the stairs and walked back to her bedroom.

Sighing heavily, she began to close the French doors to her balcony. But how could she go to sleep now? After everything that had happened? If her father wasn't going to investigate, someone had to.

I'll go out on the balcony and have another look, Winnie decided.

The moon was behind a cloud now, and the streetlights did little to throw any light on Market Square. Winnie leaned over the railing, looking left and then right, but she couldn't see anything at all. Then, off in the distance, she heard the faint blare of a truck horn.

"Snatcher's men," Winnie said, drawing in her breath. "The Boxtrolls must still be out there. They haven't gone back to their Death Cave. Maybe that means that the boy they took is still safe. Maybe he's going to be okay."

The horn blared again.

Winnie rubbed her arms to soothe the sudden goose bumps that prickled her skin, and sighed with the excitement of it all.

Chapter 6

Eggs had never run so fast, or for so long, in all his life. He wasn't sure who was having more trouble keeping up: him, or Fish and Shoe. There was barely time to stop and catch a breath, when the blare of the Red Hats' horn sounded again.

"Hark! Here come the exterminators!" howled one of the Red Hats.

Eggs didn't have time to remark to Fish and Shoe how stupid it was to repeatedly tell something you were chasing that you were chasing it. It kind of defeated the purpose.

"They're back that way. Quick, down this alley!" Eggs whispered. "Quietly!"

The trio crept down the alley, pressed as close against the wall as they could get. The voices of the Red Hat exterminators were clearly audible in the dark.

"Don't much like the sound of 'exterminators,'" said the enormous one called Trout. For a man that size, his voice was surprisingly soft. "Too negative, not heroic enough. Might give the idea that *we're* the villains."

"Huh," came Pickles's voice, which was thin and awkward like the rest of him. "Well, what about something along the lines of...exterminators of *justice!*"

"But that makes it sound like we just find justice and then exterminate *that*," Trout grumbled.

Eggs's foot brushed an old can, and he paused. But the Red Hats did not seem to have heard anything. Nearby, Eggs heard the familiar sound of someone rummaging through a trash bin.

"Sparky? Knickers?" Eggs hissed. It was probably them. They had been heading this way when Eggs made his Market Square detour.

The rummaging stopped for a moment, just as twin headlights illuminated the length of the alley. Eggs saw Knickers climbing out of the trash bin with a lady's shoe in one hand. Sparky was hoisting himself out, too, gurgling in appreciation at the shoe.

"Sparky, Knickers, *run!*" Eggs shouted. "Red Hats right behind us!"

The Boxtrolls squealed, and the shoe went flying as

Knickers and Sparky leapt off the bin and began to run. But the alley was a dead end!

"*Up!*" yelled Eggs, pointing at a fire escape.

Moments later, all five of them were on the roof, preparing to jump across a short space to the adjacent roof. Sparky and Knickers tucked themselves neatly inside their boxes, making themselves more streamlined as they sailed into the air. But it had been a long time since Eggs was able to tuck himself inside his box. To his knowledge, he was the only Boxtroll ever to outgrow his box. And no one had ever offered him a new one.

Shoe said something like "*Splerrumblegeee!*" and Eggs obliged by grabbing hold of Shoe's box as he jumped. They landed safely on the next roof with a *thud*.

"Thanks," Eggs said.

On the street, there was a screech of tires on cobblestones as the Red Hats' truck swerved around the corner into view. Gristle was driving but simultaneously had his head stuck out the window like a dog.

"I'm going fast!" Gristle announced triumphantly to the night.

Pickles, clinging to the side of the truck, fired the net gun at something.

"Awwww," Pickles wailed. "I thought I saw one!"

The truck stopped so that Pickles could collect the empty net.

From the rooftop, Eggs could see that a long gutter ended within several yards of a drainage opening in the ground that was their passage to safety.

"Quick, follow me!" Eggs said.

He slid down the gutter, landing neatly on the ground. As the Boxtrolls slid down after him, one at a time, Eggs sprinted to the drainage pipe.

"Over there!" Gristle shouted. "Getting us closer! Aim the net gun!"

"Jump!" Eggs said, not even waiting to repeat it. He plunged down the pipe, hearing Shoe mumble something as he dove in, too. Eggs curled himself up as best he could as he half tumbled and half slid down the pipe, eventually landing with a wet *plop* in the sewer.

"Not the best smell," Eggs muttered.

As each Boxtroll dropped into the sewer, the small splash shot ripples of the bad smell into the air. Eggs wrinkled his nose.

"We'll, we're safe, anyway," he said. "We'd better... Wait a minute! Where's Fish?"

Eggs and the Boxtrolls looked around wildly. Then they heard shouting overhead.

"Yes, yes, it's in the net! *We got one!*" Pickles howled.

"No!" shouted Eggs, hoisting himself up into the pipe and starting to climb toward the street.

Shoe and Sparky grabbed Eggs's feet, yanking him back.

"No, stop! He's up there! I can get him!" Eggs cried. "Let me go! I have to get Fish!"

But the Boxtrolls had Eggs firmly in their grip. They frog-marched him along the sewer until they came to one of their chutes. Gently, one of them pushed Eggs into it.

Not even a fat, tasty-looking grub brought directly to Eggs's nook could tempt him. He stared blankly at his Music Machine, listening to one of his favorite songs. Nothing was okay. Even the Music Machine wasn't playing properly. The singer and band sounded like they were being tumbled round and round in a dryer.

Shoe continued to dangle the grub in front of Eggs. When he got no response, he produced a gazillipede clutched in his other clawed hand. Eggs simply shook his head. With a sigh of resignation, Shoe popped the gazillipede into his own mouth.

"Why do we do this, Shoe?" Eggs asked. "Why do we still come back here after a night like this and make ourselves go on as if everything is normal?"

Shoe's mouth hung open in response to that question. The gazillipede seized the opportunity to crawl out of Shoe's mouth and scamper up onto the relative safety of the Boxtroll's head.

"They drag us away, and we do *nothing*," Eggs said, shaking his head wearily.

Shoe simply sat in silence. It was true, of course. Nothing could change it. The Red Hats were determined to wipe out the Boxtrolls, and they were making better progress than ever.

The permanently warped sound of the cavern clock chimed, signaling the traditional end of the Boxtroll day and summoning all to begin assembling the sleeping pile.

Shoe got up to go and waited for Eggs to get up, too.

Eggs peered out into the cavern, where Boxtrolls were beginning to stack themselves for cozy slumber. Then he looked around his nook. Lined up against one wall were Oil Can's hat and Wheels's old unicycle, which he'd had ever since their capture. Next to his Music Machine, a small bow saw lay on the ground where Fish had left it.

Fish. Big, gentle Fish. He had always been there for Eggs, looking out for him, making him laugh, teaching him to dance, helping him build his Music Machine. Rubbing his back when he had trouble getting to sleep.

Fish. Life without him seemed just impossible. Pointless.

Eggs picked up Fish's saw and placed it with Oil Can's hat and Wheels's unicycle.

"Go away," he told Shoe. "I just want to be alone."

Shoe wearily waddled over to the ledge, where he stepped into a troll-lift that whisked him toward the cavern floor.

Eggs sat down on the floor of his nook.

What can I do? he asked himself. *Fish was big and strong and kind and good, but the Red Hats caught him. We'll never win. We can't even fight.*

A corner of an album cover was sticking out from beneath the Music Machine. Eggs yanked it out. Tears sprang into his eyes when he realized what it was—his favorite Quattro Sabatinos record. The one Fish had gotten for him when he was just a tiny Boxtroll still dwarfed by his box.

Fish.

Eggs hugged the album cover to his box, then held it at arm's length, scrutinizing the four men again, with their non-yellow eyes and pink furless skin, their rounded ears, and their slender, clawless hands.

Eggs looked down at his own undersized hands.

And all at once, Eggs had an idea.

The sleeping pile was already a concerto of Boxtroll snores and sleep mumbles, though the light was still on. Shoe, who was near the top of the pile and not yet asleep, sat bolt upright and gave a squeak of fear before cowering inside his box. The thing that had so frightened him stepped forward into the dim light.

"It's only me," Eggs said. "And I've got a plan. I've just made myself a funny striped box jacket and a hat, and drawn some fur under my nose. See? I look just like one of the Quattro Sabatinos!"

Shoe and the few other Boxtrolls who had awakened just stared.

"Look, I'm going to go up there and get Fish back," Eggs declared.

Shoe peered out of his box.

"Blehbobbity mebbda mbow."

"Well, we don't know that," Eggs responded. "Either way, I've got to do something to help. At least, I've got to try. Fish would do the same for me. You know he would."

Eggs hesitated a moment. Then he sighed. He hadn't really expected anyone to volunteer to help him. Still, it would have been nice. He began to walk away, a scary flappity feeling unfolding in his belly. Suddenly, he stepped back into the light.

"Hey, guys? Do I at least kind of look like one of... them?"

Shoe and Sparky both stared at him, then exchanged a long look.

They both nodded.

"Okay," Eggs said. "I mean, that's what I thought.

I'll be fine. I just hope nobody asks me to sing."

Eggs walked slowly, but with what he hoped looked like a hero's sense of purpose, toward the Sucker-Upper, which would take him up to the Aboveground ramp. Shoe watched him go and shook his head. He lifted one stubby hand and reached up to pull the string to turn out the light. But for the first time, the sleeping pile was not high enough, and Shoe could not reach it.

"*Blerch*," Shoe said. The Boxtrolls were vanishing.

Eggs was their only hope now.

Chapter 7

For a moment, Eggs thought perhaps he'd been hit by lightning. He had only just begun to push the manhole cover up when a giant flash of light made him reel back, and then, with a rumbling sound, the manhole cover was forced shut.

"It must be a storm," Eggs said, checking his straw hat and stripy jacket to make sure his disguise was still intact. He took a moment to pull himself together. Then he gathered his strength and shoved the manhole cover up again.

Clank!

It instantly slammed shut again.

"What in the world?" wondered Eggs. He tried a third time, more tentatively lifting up the manhole cover a few inches. He heard a rumble, then *thwack!*

The hole closed again. It was like some giant hand kept coming down from the sky and shutting the lid!

"Wait a minute," Eggs told himself. He tried not to

talk to himself too much in the cavern, because some of the Boxtrolls found it odd. But there was no one here to give him the yellow fish-eye.

"Let's go over what I know. It's sleeping time for Boxtrolls, which means it is awake time for the Cheese Bits. Awake time means daylight, and moving around. So that explains the light. And the rumbling..."

Eggs remembered the exterminator vehicle the Red Hats had. Of course, other Cheese Bits had motorized wheeled vehicles, too! And most manholes opened onto the street.

"I've got to peek, and wait until there are no vehicles on the road," Eggs declared. "Yes, that's right!" It made him feel better to say it out loud, as though he had a clever friend with him who was coming up with the smart stuff, so that Eggs only had to agree.

Very cautiously, he created just a sliver of space between the cover and the manhole and peered through. Two more rumbles shuddered by, and then the way looked clear.

"Okay, now!" Eggs told himself.

He shoved the manhole cover to one side, scampered up onto the street, and kicked the cover back into place.

Then he flung one stripy sleeve over his eyes.

I'm blind! Eggs thought.

The sidewalk had been to his right when he emerged. Hoping it hadn't moved, Eggs stumbled in that direction. There was a dull roar all around him, the noise of countless voices talking and laughing and shouting at the same time. Something shoved him in one direction, then another.

Eggs pulled his hat over his eyes to shade them. The sidewalk was literally seething with Cheese Bits! Was it always like this during the day?

"Step right up, step right up!" a voice blared from behind Eggs. "Get yer picture taken with the Trubshaw baby! A personalized and humorous keepsake for this dark and dreadful day! Get yers now!"

Eggs turned around and gasped. A Cheese Bit in a funny hat and jacket was holding up a little toy figure of a small Cheese Bit that had been half covered with red paint. The man was standing in front of a tremendous picture-taking machine, flanked by two of the biggest lightbulbs Eggs had ever seen.

"Hold the Trubshaw baby for a moment, say cheese, and keep the gruesome memento for life!" sang the picture-taker man.

Wow, Eggs thought, trying not to stare at the machine, and the huge stand that held it up, and the enormous lightbulbs on either side of it. *Imagine what we could make of all those things in the Boxtroll cavern!*

There was a slight *poof* and both bulbs emitted a blinding flash of light. Eggs staggered backward. Someone hurrying in the other direction pushed against him, and Eggs found himself swept up in the crowd, like a bit of seaweed tumbling along in a wave.

He stumbled to a stop near another Cheese Bit who was holding a strange and colorful collection of bouncing balls on strings that seemed to float in the air all by themselves.

"Trubshaw Baby Day merchandise right here!" called the man. "We got pennants! We got bookmarks! We got sunglasses! We got T-shirts! And what better way to observe this tragic theft of a bouncing baby than with a lovely bouncing balloon?"

Eggs, entranced by the balloons, reached up and poked at the one nearest him. It bobbed and rotated on its string, and Eggs drew back, horrified. The balloon had the grotesque, crudely drawn face of a Boxtroll on it.

All the balloons did.

What's wrong with these people? Eggs wondered as he hurried away. If some dreadful tragedy had taken place involving a small Cheese Bit named Trup Chaw or whatever it was, why did everyone look so darn happy?

Hanging on to his hat with one hand, Eggs pushed through the crowd until he spotted the relative safety of a lamppost. He made his way over to it and wrapped one arm around it like he'd found a long-lost relative in the crowd. Pulling himself up and out of the way, Eggs was finally able to catch his breath.

The crowd seemed to stretch in every direction. Eggs watched the mass of people seethe and surge like a blob sharing a single consciousness. Over the *bler-bler-bler* of their voices, Eggs heard something else: The sound of a single bell ringing. Eggs searched the crowd for the source of the sound. His eyes widened and his mouth dropped.

I can't be seeing what I think I'm seeing, Eggs thought. *That can't be real.*

Waddling through the crowd, ringing a huge hand-bell, was an old Boxtroll.

"Hey!" Eggs called.

But the crowd was too loud, and the Boxtroll did not hear him, or pretended he did not. Eggs jumped from the safety of the lamppost and pushed through the throng, trying to catch up to the Boxtroll.

He stopped at a large stage set up on the street. It was fronted by a wooden wall that reached the ground. The Boxtroll pressed on a panel of the wall, which swung open like a little door. As Eggs jumped forward, the Boxtroll disappeared right before his eyes, but not before Eggs got close enough to see it was actually a Cheese Bit wearing a Boxtroll costume.

"Hey!" Eggs yelled again, but the fake Boxtroll was gone.

Curiouser and curiouser, Eggs thought. *Aboveground is a very strange place.*

He turned to head back to the lamppost—he needed some air, and the crowd was making him feel dizzy and disoriented. But something was happening.

The crowd was magically parting in front of Eggs. Overhead, the sound of a musical horn rang out, and the crowd drew back even farther. At Eggs's back was the stage, and ahead of him was an empty avenue created by the space of thousands of Cheese Bits making room. Making room for...what? Or whom?

Everyone seemed to be bending over and looking hard at the ground now, as if they'd all simultaneously lost their contact lenses.

This is really weird, Eggs thought. *Maybe I'd better—*

Before he could finish the thought, a big, burly Cheese Bit darted forward and grabbed him.

"Hey, kid, what's the matter with you? You got to bow down—the White Hats are coming!"

Eggs yanked his arm free from the big Cheese Bit. At the same time, he noticed he was, in fact, the only living creature present among the masses who was not bowing deeply.

This doesn't seem to be a good time to call attention to myself, Eggs thought, hastily mimicking the deep, head-to-knees bows of the crowd.

The horns blared again, and Eggs peeked.

A procession of Cheese Bits in impossibly white hats was marching by. The parting crowd bowed and cheered; some of them even pretended to weep in awe.

"We are not worthy!" cried a woman.

"Good morning, fine sirs!" called someone.

"Looking very noble today, sirs!" another enthusiastically exclaimed.

"You were all in my dreams last night, sirs!" cried a third.

To Eggs's surprise, a very old and frail-looking Cheese Bit, who reminded him a little of Sweets, tottered forward toward the marching White Hats.

"Lord Portley-Rind, sir! Please! The factory was condemned and I lost me job, lost me home, have no food! We need your help! Please, sir!"

The one called Lord Portley-Rind, a large, red-haired man in an immaculate uniform covered with shiny pins and medals, glanced at the old Cheese Bit.

"How simply dreadful," Lord Portley-Rind said without missing a step. "Certainly, you shall have help, my good fellow. Someone get that man a bit of cheddar."

A servant closely trailing Lord Portley-Rind nodded and presented a small cube of cheddar to the old man.

"Thank you, sir, I—wait, that's *it*? This is all I get?" the old man exclaimed, staring in disbelief at the little square of cheese in his hand.

But the White Hats had already swept past.

"A mouthful of cheese isn't going to help that man," Eggs muttered.

Already, another bedraggled-looking man had jumped forward.

"Your Lordship, the city's sewers are overflowing and the streets are crumbling! Me own granny tripped on a pothole and broke her hip! And, oh, sirs, where is the children's hospital you promised us last year on Trubshaw Baby Day?"

Lord Portley-Rind made a swatting gesture at the man, as if he were a housefly.

"Good people," he called in his thundering voice. "Much as we would love to assist and placate each and every one of you with cheese, I must remind you that this is not a day for business or complaints! Today is a day of remembrance, a day when we look back on our town's darkest hour, a day when…I say…a day when… Cue the music!"

On command, a burst of music erupted. It seemed to Eggs's ringing ears to be coming from every direction at once. Lord Portley-Rind seemed to be scanning the crowd, looking for someone. Instinctively, Eggs shrank lower into his bow.

He isn't looking for me—he can't be, Eggs told himself firmly. *I'm in disguise. I'm the fifth Sabatino brother. I am the fifth Sabatino brother.*

As Eggs worked on hypnotizing himself, a chorus of *ooh*s and *oh, my*s and *oo-la-la*s rang out.

"Ah, there she is now!" boomed Lord Portley-Rind. "Make way for the lovely Madame Frou Frou! To the stage, my good people, to the stage!"

The crowd surged obligingly, coming together and pushing toward the stage, where Eggs was still standing. Someone pointed.

"Look at the curtain! Someone's pushed a megaphone through!" a voice shouted.

Eggs turned to look at what everyone else was looking at. A long funnel had appeared where two sections of curtain met, center stage. A sing-song yet somewhat familiar voice came out of it.

"Ladies and gents, children of all ages! From Crackerslovakia—a town destroyed by Boxtrolls, so don't bother looking for it—our guest, who's been through it all but is here to enthrall! That's right, she's gone through perdition, and now she's dishin'! Yessiree, from a ravage land, she'll tell you firsthand!"

The curtain shifted slightly, and Eggs got a glimpse of the hand holding the megaphone. It was a big, hairy hand with lumpy knuckles, and the oversized wrist was straining inside a tight, lacy sleeve.

"That's bizarre," Eggs mumbled.

"And so, my good people," the voice continued, "without any further ado, I give you the divine *Madame Frou Frou!*"

The crowd went wild, hollering and clapping and stamping their feet on the cobblestones. The curtains parted, and a very large, elaborately coiffed woman in a luxuriously appointed full-length gown stepped forward, blowing kisses at the giddy crowd with her heavily painted lips.

"My daaaaaaaaaaalinks!" the woman cried in a husky, loud voice. "Tank you, tank you!" Behind her, off to one side, the White Hats had gathered and were bowing and blushing and making reverent little gestures at the woman.

"Looking even lovelier than usual today, my *dear* Frou Frou!" Lord Portley-Rind said. He was blocking Lord Boulanger's view, and the old man tried to scoot his wheelchair out front, but Lord Portley-Rind aimed a discreet kick and diverted the chair's trajectory. He lunged forward to grab Madame Frou Frou's hand.

"Oh, Lord Portley-Rind, you old so-and-so, you are *too* much!" Madame Frou Frou said with a girlish giggle amplified by an unexpected rumble of baritone that made her fleshy jowls quiver. "Or maybe you're *just* enough! Meeeeow, purrrrrrrrrrrrr..."

Madame Frou Frou attempted to retrieve her hand, but Lord Portley-Rind was hanging on for dear life. Finally, after more giggling and wiggling, the lady playfully smacked Lord Portley-Rind in the nose with her fan. Momentarily startled, he let go of her hand, and Madame Frou Frou hurried downstage with resoundingly loud footsteps.

"My dear people of Cheesebridge, it is soooooo good of you to come and hear my sad, sad tale. Of course, you all know how the vicious Boxtroll *beasts* devoured my beloved Crackerslovakia, leaving me a woman without a home! Oh, the infamy—those villains consumed my native town brick by brick and baby by baby! As Gouda is my witness, those Boxtrolls *ate. It. All!*"

"Booo!" roared the crowd. "Villains! Monsters! *Revenge!*"

Eggs went pale, shrinking back from the sheer hatred in the voices of the townspeople.

This is crazy! he thought. *A Boxtroll wouldn't hurt a fly! Well, except to eat it. Anyone in their right mind can see that the real monsters are the creeps in the hats! Red Hats and White, they're all horrible!*

"And now I can do nothing but travel the world, warning other towns to beware the monsters, so that they do not share my poor Crackerslovakia's fate! Because, mark my words, they will return," Madame Frou Frou concluded, wiping what must have been an excessively small tear from her eye with a giant lacy handkerchief.

The crowd cheered now. Eggs stared at them dismally, wondering how so many people could have fallen victim to such a great pack of lies. He caught a glimpse of a pale-faced young girl with red hair, and he did a double take.

I know that girl! Eggs thought. Then he reprimanded himself. *Don't be silly, Eggs. You're a Boxtroll. You don't know any girls.*

"Now quiet down, people!" Madame Frou Frou commanded shrilly. "For it is now time for you to join the story. Cheesebridge has had its own bitter taste of tragedy at the teeth of the Boxtrolls, has it not? And that is why we are here today—to recount the sad story of the Trubshaw baby abduction!"

"No, we can't—it's too painful. But if we must, hooray!" came a jumble of voices.

"But first, as most of you know, I work *with* my audience, not *for* them. I require a helper from amongst you. Do I have…*a volunteer!*"

A small throng of well-dressed Cheese Bit children shoved their way to the front of the crowd, all of them shouting. Eggs could see that the girl with the red hair had raised her hand high and was now leaping and waving in an attempt to make herself seen.

"Now, the rule is you must put your hand in the air, and I don't see any hands…." Madame Frou Frou scolded the children.

"My hand was up!" shouted the red-haired girl. "That means I'm the volunteer!"

Without waiting for Madame Frou Frou to answer, the red-haired girl climbed up on the stage and stood next to her, gazing out over the crowd.

Eggs's mouth dropped open. He suddenly realized why she looked familiar.

It was the Cheese Bit girl from Market Square, the girl he'd come face-to-face with the night before. The girl who had called after him.

The one who had called Eggs a name he'd never been called before in his life. A strange name that felt like his own box, familiar but the wrong...size.

Boy.

Chapter 8

From his position very close to the front of the stage, Eggs could hear the red-haired girl talking as Madame Frou Frou tied a bonnet around her head and attempted to stick a pacifier in her mouth.

"Did you hear me? I said I saw a *boy* with some Boxtrolls! Don't you think you should tell the audience that—"

"Bite down, Miss Portley-Rind," Madame Frou Frou commanded, pushing the pacifier into the girl's mouth.

"Issh Winnie," the girl corrected. Madame Frou Frou shrugged.

"Either way, stick to the script, kid," she commanded, with a rumbling hint of threat in her voice. "Music, please!"

Eggs watched in growing disbelief as Madame Frou Frou embarked on a grotesque song-and-dance number.

"Oh, not too long agoooo, and not too far awaaayyyyy, the little Trubshaw child was happily at plaaaaay...." she began.

Someone jumped onto the stage and roared. Eggs recognized him as one of the Red Hats, dressed in a ridiculous costume that was supposed to pass for a Boxtroll suit.

"Roar!" the Red Hat yelled, advancing on Winnie, who was pretending to be sleeping like a baby.

Oh, please, Eggs thought.

He covered his face with his hands but could not block out the blare of Madame Frou Frou's voice or the words of her repulsive song.

"Up came a monster, a man-eating beast! He stole that poor boy for a late-night feast! With ten-inch talons, with blood-soaked teeth, it took that poor baby to its caves underneath!"

The crowd booed and hissed, and some of them shouted, "Look out, baby Trubshaw!"

"Help! Father, save me!" called a different voice.

It was the girl! Eggs opened his eyes and almost lunged forward. But there she was, still onstage, being pushed toward a trapdoor by the costumed Red Hat.

She isn't in danger, thought Eggs. *She's…she's…she's acting. I thought they were supposed to be commemorating a tragedy. How disgusting.*

As the girl slipped through the trapdoor and disappeared from view, an awkwardly tall and gangly Red Hat came onstage, howling like a distraught father. Madame Frou-Frou pointed a heavily jeweled hand at him.

"The poor father woke. Oh, he cried, cried, cried! All 'cause he forgot to lock his babe inside!"

"Tell 'em, Mr. Pickles!" someone cheered, clapping.

Pickles dropped to his knees onstage, howling like a tone-deaf coyote auditioning for *Cheesebridge Idol.*

"Noooo! Trubshaw baby, noooooo! You were my only child! And I am so distraught and confused by fear that I have staggered out into the streets searching under every rock for you, forgetting that I now render myself vulnerable to the vicious beasts!"

"Behind you," shouted someone. "It's that brute Gristle being a Boxtroll—look out!"

Madame Frou Frou stepped forward and raised her hefty arms in the air.

"The sun went down, but father kept on lookin'.

So the Boxtrolls grabbed *him,* to do some more cookin'!" she droned.

Gristle pounced on Pickles and dragged him toward the trapdoor, launching him into it with one well-aimed kick to the behind.

Just when Eggs thought the spectacle could not get any worse, or more offensive, Gristle began prancing around, rubbing his stomach and drooling, as if he were preparing for a raw and bloody meal. The audience bellowed its disapproval, and Madame Frou Frou drew herself up to her full height so her singing could be heard over the roar.

"They baked father and son over a fiery pit! And iced their eyeballs for a banana split! They pickled their tongues and jerkied their skin and distilled all their blood into bathtub *gin!*"

Gristle yanked open the trapdoor, reached in, and pulled out a bunch of extremely fake-looking bones, which he crammed into his mouth.

"Yum! Nom nom nom!" he said.

Eggs stamped his foot.

"Boxtrolls are bug-atarians, you idiot!" Eggs shouted, letting his temper get the better of him. "And nobody actually says 'nom nom nom' when they eat!"

Fortunately for Eggs, there was far too much noise for him to be heard.

"Boxtroll, be gone!" Madame Frou Frou bellowed, rushing at Gristle and beating him over the head with her fan.

"Ow! Ow!" Gristle protested. "You are hurting my feelings."

He lay down and covered his head with his hands, and Madame Frou Frou climbed on top of him, forcing a faint *ooooo* sound to escape his lips.

"So fellows, lock your doors, and gals, lock your gate. Please heed my warning, before it's too late! Fathers, hide your mothers, and mothers, hide your kid! Or you'll all of you end up just like that Trubshaw baby did!"

The crowd went wild, cheering and roaring.

"Bravo!" they called. "Encore!"

I've got to get out of here, Eggs told himself. *I think I'm going to be sick.*

It made no sense to go toward the crowd. While everyone was busy clapping and hollering for the bowing Madame Frou Frou, Eggs carefully made his way around the stage, emerging with relief on a vacant patch of street behind it.

The situation was much worse than he'd thought, Eggs realized. *These Cheese Bits are all suffering from delusions!* he said to himself. *I don't think there's anything I can do to help anyone....I ought to just go home.*

Out of the corner of his eye, Eggs saw movement. A small door at the back of the stage structure opened, and the red-haired girl who called herself Winnie emerged, brushing off her clothing. Eggs tried to make himself as small and unnoticeable as possible.

Winnie didn't look as if she'd noticed him. She headed off down the street, and after a moment, when it seemed no one else was going to show up, Eggs decided to follow her.

Winnie examined her reflection, taking a long time to fix and then refix her hair.

Yes, there he was again—Winnie could clearly see the striped jacket reflected in the mirror.

He is following me, Winnie thought. *But why? Is he one of Father's minions, or merely a pickpocket?*

Trying to act as casual as possible, Winnie began walking again, humming to herself and looking in each store window and at each stand she passed. When she saw a stall displaying brightly colored ribbons and necklaces, she stopped and pretended to examine the merchandise.

"Ooh, soft," she said out loud, fingering one of the ribbons. "And such colors—almost good enough to eat!"

She heard a rustle and glanced under lowered eyelids to one side, where a figure in a badly made striped jacket was also now touching the ribbons. To her astonishment, he pulled one of the ribbons toward his mouth, tried to take a bite of it, then spat it back onto the table.

What a weirdo!

Winnie hastened away. He was no minion—all her father's lackeys were far too well-bred to behave so rudely. He must be a street thief.

But as fast as Winnie walked, the footsteps kept pace with her.

Maybe I can't outrun him, she thought. *But if he knew he was stalking the daughter of a White Hat, he'd probably trip over his own feet trying to escape.*

She rounded a corner, then doubled back and stepped boldly onto the sidewalk, stopping right in front of her surprised follower.

"*Aha!*" Winnie shouted, triumphantly. "Caught you! What are you doing? Why are you following me?"

The thief looked around wildly, caught sight of an old barrel resting against a building, and dove inside it.

"Uh, hello? I saw you go in there," Winnie said. "And unless that thing has a false bottom, you're not getting away. What is your deal, anyway? You are the worst pickpocket I've ever seen. And what's with the Ringo Sabatino outfit?"

He just stared her from the barrel, his hat drooping down over one eye.

"Whatever. Suit yourself," Winnie said, tossing a coin into the barrel. "Here—get yourself a copy of *Pickpocketing for Weirdos.*"

She walked away, trying to swallow her disappointment. Whenever it seemed like something exciting might be happening to her, it always ended up being stupid.

"Wuhhhh," Winnie heard. "Ahhhewww..."

She turned around.

The pickpocket had climbed out of the barrel and was trying to say something.

"English," Winnie said loudly. "I only speak English."

"I saw…you. I saw you. Last night."

Winnie froze. Truth be told, that sounded totally creepy. Unless…unless he meant…

"I saw you and then they took Fish," he added.

Winnie took several steps forward and pulled off his hat.

"Hey, wait a minute," she said. "Yeah! You were the one with the Boxtrolls last night!"

Eggs intuitively took a step back. Every single Cheese Bit he'd encountered considered the Boxtrolls to be mad, bad, and dangerous to know. But Winnie was just standing there, her head cocked to one side and her expression curious.

"Yes," Eggs said.

"I knew it!" Winnie exclaimed excitedly. *"I knew it! No one would believe me! I can't believe you got away! I'm so relieved! I wanted to help, but no one would listen to me! How did you escape?"*

"We went underground," Eggs said. "But they got Fish."

"They dragged you down to their Death Cave?" Winnie asked, her eyes huge.

"Huh?" Eggs blinked in confusion.

"Were there mountains of baby bones and rivers of blood? Oh, don't answer that—you must be suffering from post-traumatic stress disorder. You could be in shock. You need a blanket! Anyway, it was probably pitch-black except for the glow of the cook fire. So, did they eat your family?"

"My family is—"

"Did they make you watch? Did you hear bones snapping? I'm tougher than I look—tell me *everything*!" Winnie pleaded.

What is wrong with this person? Eggs thought, freaked out and practically in tears with frustration. *Is she just like the rest of them? How can anyone get a Cheese Bit's attention?*

Seized with a sudden impulse, Eggs grabbed Winnie's arm, lifted it to his mouth, and bit it.

"Ow!" Winnie yelled. "You bit me!"

"I need to find the men with the red hats," Eggs said loudly.

"You bit me with your *mouth*!"

"Where do I find the men with the red hats?" Eggs demanded.

Winnie looked taken aback.

"I...What? You mean the Boxtroll exterminators? They're a bunch of coarsely bred louts. Why would you want to bother with them?"

"Where *are* they?" Eggs cried.

Winnie put her hands up.

"Okay, relax. Geez. The Red Hats all live on Curd's Way. See that street there? That's Milk Street. Just stay on it for a long time—eventually, it turns into Curd."

Eggs looked up at the street sign, then nodded. He brushed past Winnie and took off down Milk Street. Then he stopped and turned around.

"That stuff isn't true, you know," he said. "It's ridiculous. And we do *not* eat babies!"

Then he raced away as Winnie stared after him.

"What's not true?" she called. "And how do you... Did you say '*we*'? Did you just say, '*We* don't eat babies'?"

Eggs did not even slow down.

None of this makes sense, Winnie thought. *There's something up with that kid, and why is he dressed that way, and why did he eat a ribbon and dive into a barrel, and why does he talk like he...like he* knows *the Boxtrolls?*

Without bothering to mull it over any further, Winnie picked up her skirts and ran after the boy as fast as she could.

Chapter 9

There was nothing there but a big old run-down building.

Eggs looked around.

Well, what did you expect? he asked himself. *That the Red Hats would all just be standing here, waiting for you to find them?*

Of course, the girl might have been lying. She was a Cheese Bit, after all, and that's what Cheese Bits did.

But there's something about her, Eggs thought. *She doesn't seem like the others—not exactly.*

Then Eggs heard something, just for a fraction of a moment. He spun around and saw nothing. No one. But his heart was suddenly beating a mile a minute. It might just have been his imagination kicking into over-drive. But Eggs didn't think so. He knew that sound too well.

"That definitely sounded like a Boxtroll," he said,

nodding. And not just any old Boxtroll voice. It sounded very much like a Boxtroll who had just dropped something on his foot or bonked his head. It was the sound of a Boxtroll saying a thing that meant *ouch*.

"It had to have come from that building," Eggs said. "There's nothing else around."

A sign over the door was weathered and warped and difficult to read, but Eggs could make out the word FAC-TORY. The door itself at one time had had something painted on it. Eggs squinted at the peeling, rust-colored outline, then realized what the painting had been. A red hat. Clearly, this was the place.

Near the door, a stack of empty wooden crates lay in a jumble on the ground.

Eggs crept over and grabbed one, then another, expertly creating steps and a platform onto which he could climb. The windows were smeared with filth, but a small crescent had been broken out of one, and Eggs peered through it. At first, he eyes could not make out anything in the darkness, but he heard voices.

"I'm poking it with a stick, Mr. Pickles," someone said. "Hey, you! *I am poking you with a stick!*"

"Don't waste your breath, Mr. Gristle. He don't speak English. Now, Mr. Trout, do you ever get to wondering what they think about?"

"Oh, I imagine they're evaluating their life choices, Mr. Pickles," came the reply.

"Right you may be, Trout, pondering as how they chose to be dirty, disgusting monsters instead of fine, upstanding heroes such as ourselves."

"You are *all wrong*!" came another voice, from deeper within the factory.

Eggs ducked, then raised himself up a little. He heard the sound of footsteps echoing off the factory walls.

"Mr. Snatcher! We wasn't expecting you!"

Eggs pressed one eye to the little hole in the glass.

He could see the Red Hat boss now, striding into what seemed to be a large chamber full of boxes.

"Listen and learn," Snatcher said. "A Boxtroll cannot *choose* a lifestyle, because a Boxtroll does not *aspire* to be anything more than a weak, flesh-eating pest. Now, a *man*, on the other hand, can and should choose to change his own life. Our dreams are in our grasp! We should grasp them, snatch them, claim our dreams, our *destiny,* and *shove it down everyone else's throat!"*

There was a brief silence.

"Throat," Gristle repeated.

"Fine words, fine words, Mr. Snatcher. I daresay that's why you're the boss," Pickles mumbled.

"I should say so," Snatcher growled. "So, you will all agree, gentlemen, that the best way to walk in the shoes of those we aspire to be is to emulate them. Mr. Pickles? Fetch the—"

"Shoes?" asked Pickles, his voice overlapping with Trout's suggesting, "Clogs?"

There was a brief pause.

"Bat?" suggested Gristle.

Eggs's eyes had adjusted well enough to see that Gristle was swinging something in the air as Pickles and Trout ducked.

"No, the *cheese!"* Snatcher's voice thundered.

The crate Eggs was standing on shifted slightly. He jumped to the ground, rearranged the crates, and climbed up them again. Now he could see Snatcher and his Red Hats sitting down at a long table. Each of them held what looked like an old paper airplane in his hand.

"Ready, then? Gentlemen, don your white hats."

At Snatcher's command, the men lifted their hands to their heads, whisked off their red hats, and placed the white paper things on their heads like cheap, lopsided crowns.

"Are you sure about this, boss?" asked Pickles. "It feels wrong....Maybe we've all had one too many slices of cheese, and you know what that does to you, know what I mean?"

Snatcher slammed his fist onto the table so hard that even Eggs jumped a little.

"Unless you are referring to the unifying power of cheese and its ability to unite respectful men in brotherhood, I most certainly do *not* know what you mean!" he barked.

"Nope, me neither, but what you said, that's what I meant," Pickles mumbled.

"Then let us begin," Snatcher said grandly.

Eggs watched curiously as Trout opened a small wrapped bundle, his hands trembling. He broke off a morsel of the bundle's contents and put it on a plate. It was a tiny orange bit that looked like cheddar cheese.

"What are they doing?" Eggs wondered.

Trout put three smaller pieces of orange on the

three remaining plates and lined them up. Then he pushed on the table until it slowly began to turn, like a giant spool. After a great deal of creaking and groaning from both the table and Trout, the table revolved just far enough to deposit a plate in front of each man.

Eggs watched as Snatcher ceremoniously lifted a piece of cheese to his lips, reverently closed his eyes, then placed it on his tongue. He emitted little sounds of delight as he chewed. It seemed to go on forever. Eggs had never seen anyone take so long to eat one bite of anything.

"Aromatic, yes? Or perhaps a hint of oak, and an undertone of a mother's smile on a warm spring day? Why, this cheese is positively, er, big words, chummy banter, very fine indeed."

"Um...you've got some..." Pickles pointed at Snatcher's face. Even from Eggs's vantage point at the window, he could see large red blotches breaking out all over Snatcher's skin.

"He's got the Cheese Fits," Pickles whispered loudly to Trout. "Fetch the leeches!"

Snatcher looked around. His face was beginning to swell, too: His lips looked like little sausages and his eyes had become mere slits.

"Blere izzh he thowink?" Snatcher snapped. "Bore cheethe?"

"Oh, boss, I don't think you should—" Pickles began.

But Snapper had already forced another piece of cheese into his rapidly swelling mouth.

He must be allergic, Eggs said to himself. *This is probably a good time for me to have a look around in there, while they're all distracted.*

Over the window, a large, tunnel-shaped air duct was bolted to the building, leading up and then through the wall. Eggs had no difficulty scampering up the inside of it as it wasn't all that different from some of the small chutes in the Boxtroll cavern. When the air duct leveled out, the air became stale and dank. He could hear muffled, raised voices.

"I wath bawn thew eath cheethe!" Snatcher was shouting. "I belong with the cheethe elite!"

"You're not wrong about that, boss," came Pickles's voice.

"Spot on," Trout agreed.

Inching forward, Eggs could see dim light ahead. Wriggling on his stomach, he maneuvered himself to the edge of the air duct. The large, decrepit factory room spread out below him. But there was something hanging in the air, some kind of crate or elevator that was blocking Eggs's view.

What is that? he wondered, scooting forward a little more and squinting to focus his eyes.

Then he gasped audibly. The object hanging in the air was not a crate but a cage! And there was something inside the cage. Some*one*. A sweetly lumpy head and doggedly pointy ears that made Eggs think of…

It was Fish!!!

Without a second thought, Eggs launched himself through the air and grasped a chain that went from floor to ceiling. He clung there silently, praying none of the Red Hats happened to look up.

"I belong in the Tathting Room on velvet pillowth, thampling the finetht cheetheth, and all the people bowing down to me and admiring my white hat!"

"Now, don't get yourself all worked up," Trout advised.

"Use your breathing," Pickles advised.

Carefully, Eggs shimmied down the chain and dropped quietly onto a crate in a shadowy corner. He peeked into the room and saw Snatcher climbing onto the wooden table, while Trout held up a jar of black, wiggling leeches.

"If you'd just lend me your face for a moment, boss," Trout said.

"Thtand back, peathantth! You dare lay a finger on your king? And I thould be king and would be king if not for the thcoundrel Portley-Rind."

From the crate, Eggs had an even better view of Fish in his cage. While Snatcher continued to vent, and the Red Hats continued to agree with every word he said, Eggs crept cautiously to the cage, grabbed hold of the bars, and hoisted himself up, making sure to keep on the side of the cage not visible to the Red Hats.

"Fish!" he whispered.

The Boxtroll turned, and for a moment Eggs thought he'd made a mistake, that this Boxtroll, with its lifeless, hazy yellow eyes, was not his old friend. But then Fish recognized Eggs, and his eyes grew wide.

"Ahhhh!" Fish exclaimed. Eggs shushed him. Fish instantly dove into his box. The momentum caused the cage to begin to rotate slowly on its chain.

"Father alwayth thaid if you work hard, you get a

white hat!" Snatcher bellowed. "And what did he get? Nothing! Ath for me, I've worked my hump off for thith thtupid town, wading through the garbage, cha-thing thothe monthterth. What hath that fat Portley-Rind ever done but gobble up cheethe and ruin the government!"

"You'd better hurry up and get those leeches on him before we lose him," Pickles muttered.

Eggs reached down and unlocked the catch to the door of the cage. Hearing the sound, Fish peeped out of his box.

"Okay, follow me. And hurry!" Eggs whispered.

Taking Fish by the hand, Eggs leapt from the cage down to the crate, pulling Fish with him.

"*Thtop!*" Snatcher's voice thundered, and Eggs froze, his heart hammering. "Thtop the world from thpinning!"

Snatcher was staggering around on the table, which had begun to spin.

"Come on down from there, boss," Pickles said. "Just take it easy. Everything is going to be fine."

"Trout, I command you to give me that bag of cheethe!" Snatcher said, stumbling backward and plummeting off the table. He hit the floor with a tremendous crash.

"He's cheese-drunk," Eggs whispered to Fish. "Might be some kind of allergic reaction, too. Listen, Fish. We've got to get back up there to that air duct. Quickly, while they're too crazy to notice."

Snatcher was continuing to shout and bray like an enraged donkey as Pickles and Trout slowly inched toward him with the bottle of leeches. Eggs saw Pickles lunge.

"Got him!" Pickles yelled. "Do it now, Trout! Do it now!"

"I'm putting leeches on your face!" Gristle cried triumphantly.

Fish just didn't seem able to do anything, so Eggs hoisted him onto his own back and began shimmying up a pipe that led to the ceiling. At the top, Eggs was able to get himself and Fish onto a wide rafter that led to within feet of the air duct they needed to crawl through to escape.

There were strange grunts and sucking sounds coming from below. Eggs snuck a look to see that the leeches were sucking the swelling right out of

Snatcher's face, then dropping to the floor, engorged and squirming.

"Oh. That feels better," Snatcher said. "Uh, what were we about to do?"

"We was gonna open the factory floor and put that new Boxtroll to work," Trout said.

"Quite right," Snatcher agreed. "Open the factory floor!"

Pickles pushed a huge lever, and a large section of the floor began to open, revealing a dark pit below.

"We've got to go!" Eggs whispered urgently. From the rafter, he propelled himself and Fish onto the hanging cage, and from there, gathering all his strength and combining it with the momentum of the swinging cage, he managed to toss Fish into the air duct. Eggs then stretched himself toward the duct. He had one foot on the edge of the duct and one foot still on the cage when he happened to look down.

"Retrieve the new Boxtroll!" Snatcher commanded.

There was a series of gasps and exclamations.

"Gone!"

"Where?"

"How?"

Fish made an urgent sound for Eggs to get his other leg into the air duct so they could escape. But Eggs was paralyzed, staring down, hardly able to believe his eyes. When the factory floor was rolled back, it revealed a dark pit full of machines and blurry shapes. Suddenly, one of the shapes at the end of a chain came into focus.

"Oil Can!" Eggs cried with wild disbelief. "You're alive!"

Chapter 10

There was a sudden babbling of excited voices, and Eggs realized that at the end of every chain there was a Boxtroll. "Books! Sparky! Knickers!"

The air filled with the sound of Boxtrolls calling out to him. And then another voice was added to the mix—a deep, hoarse, distinctly un-Boxtrollian voice.

"Eggs?"

Above his friends, Eggs saw a strange creature hanging upside down from one of the chains. He was very furry like a Boxtroll, but he had small pink ears and clawless hands like a Cheese Bit. Some of his face was pink, too, but the rest was covered by thatches of long fur on top of his head and around his mouth.

"Look, up there!" Snatcher shouted.

Eggs looked down and realized with dismay that Snatcher was pointing right at him.

Snatcher was staring intently at Eggs's face, his eyes narrowed.

"What the—it can't be! No! It's not possible!" Snatcher exclaimed.

"Why, yes, he's got our Boxtroll. Oy, you! Give it back!" Pickles called to Eggs.

Snatcher gave Pickles a vicious shove.

"Don't just stand there—go and *get* him! Confuse him, frighten him!"

Gristle took off running while Trout ran to the levers in the factory floor. He gave one lever a yank, and the cage on which Eggs still had one of his feet jerked up into the air. Eggs glimpsed Fish tumbling out of sight into the air duct.

Trout slammed the lever the other way, and the cage, with Eggs, plummeted to the floor as the floor continued to close over the pit. Eggs barely had time to launch himself through the air and onto a rafter.

"You!" Snatcher bellowed. "Ten years, and *now* you show up?"

Beneath him, the precious upturned faces of his Boxtroll friends disappeared as the floor closed over the pit.

"Why are you doing this?" Eggs hollered. "Box-trolls don't hurt anyone. You've no right! You've got to let them go!"

"Because I need them!" Snatcher declared. "Those Boxtrolls are my ticket to a white hat!"

Pickles and Gristle were running back and forth, trying to sort out a plan of attack on Eggs. Pickles fumbled with the net gun, and Gristle leapt onto the nearest hanging cage.

"Going up, Trout!" Gristle yelled.

Trout nodded and threw another lever. The cage smoothly ascended to the rafters, and Gristle jumped onto one. He was just feet from Eggs now, surveying him and grinning wild-eyed. He held his bat in one hand.

"Batter up!" Gristle sang.

Eggs scampered across the rafter. Down below, Pickles was aiming the net gun directly at him.

"Shoot him! Shoot him, Pickles," Snatcher bawled.

"I'm trying! Hey, you—could you stop moving for a minute?" Pickles called.

Eggs began to backtrack, but he found Gristle blocking his way, an ugly smile on his face. Gristle raised his bat at the same time Pickles aimed the gun and began to squeeze the trigger.

"I'm not going to let you kill the Boxtrolls!" Eggs called defiantly. "I'm not going to let you hurt my friends. I think you're all evil!"

"Well, I don't care what you think," Snatcher snapped. "You're not even supposed to be alive. The plan was to kill the Trubshaw baby!"

"Trubshaw...baby????"

Everyone began looking around for the source of the new voice. Eggs saw her first, standing in the open doorway of the factory.

Winnie stared up at Eggs, a half smile on her face.

Maybe he did have a chance of getting out of this after all.

"I *knew* there was something strange about you!" she called. "My intuition is very good. Did you even—?"

Winnie's voice fell away when she became aware of the Red Hats. Gristle still held his bat high in the air, ready to smash Eggs to a pulp, and Pickles was still pointing the net gun at him.

"Oh, dear. Have I interrupted something? I did knock, you know," Winnie said, narrowing her eyes.

"Why, my dear Miss Portley-Rind," Snatcher said nervously. "Does your, uh, father by any chance know that you are here?"

"Of course not," Winnie said. "But I can't wait to see the look on his face when I tell him I found the Trubshaw baby *alive and well*!"

Eggs looked down at the mass of Boxtrolls. Was there a baby in there, too? How dreadful!

Snatcher sighed wearily.

"Gentlemen, seize her."

Before Winnie realized what was happening, she was surrounded by Red Hats.

"Sorry about this, miss," Trout grumbled as he grabbed her.

"Unhand me, sir!" Winnie shrieked.

"Sadly, the town will learn that the Boxtrolls claimed another innocent victim today," Snatcher said. "That would be you."

Eggs heard the sharp *blam* of a net gun being fired. He ducked, and a ball of net flew past him. Eggs grabbed a chain, dodged Gristle and his bat, and swung down to the factory floor. Trout was holding Winnie in front of him like a shield, but Eggs's feet slammed into his shoulders, and the Red Hat went tumbling.

"Quick, to the door!" Eggs cried, pulling her along.

Outside, in the sunlight, Winnie stopped to catch her breath and stare at Eggs.

"What exactly have you gotten me into?" she asked.

"No time! Run!" Eggs ordered.

There was a crash as Gristle burst through a window, and moments later Snatcher, Pickles, and Trout came running out the door.

In one direction there was block after block of nothing. And in the other direction was the Red Hats' exterminator truck.

"Come on!" Eggs cried.

They ran to the truck and dove inside.

"Now what?" asked Winnie.

Eggs stared at her. He hadn't thought that far ahead.

"Try pushing that. Or that. Or try turning that key."

Winnie did as he said, and suddenly the engine roared to life. The truck took off so fast, Eggs almost went flying out of his seat.

"Sorry," Winnie said, gripping the wheel, her eyes huge. "I'm a pampered eleven-year-old-girl. I don't drive much."

They careered around the side of the building, where Eggs saw a familiar box.

"Wait!" he cried.

He opened the door and called urgently, "Fish! Over here!"

The box suddenly grew a head, arms, and legs. Fish did not need to be told a second time. He jumped into the truck, and Winnie floored it.

"Now what?" Winnie asked again.

"Here, wedge the gas pedal down with my shoe," Eggs told her. "As soon as the truck rounds the corner of the factory, we'll jump out. The Red Hats will be running toward the truck, and we can get away!"

It worked like a charm. As Winnie, Eggs, and Fish tore away from the truck, it continued to hurtle toward the front of the factory, where the shouting Red Hats were waiting. The ruse only bought them a few minutes, but by the time Eggs could hear Snatcher's voice barking and braying on the street, they were in the manhole and he was pulling the lid closed.

"*Where* are they?" Eggs heard Snatcher yell. He must have come to a stop almost directly over the manhole.

"Did we lose 'em?" Pickles asked. "That don't make no sense. That'd be evil prevailing over good!"

"You idiots," Snatcher snapped. "If Lord Portley-

Rind finds out the Trubshaw boy is alive, it will ruin everything I have worked so hard for!"

"Quite right. Everything we have worked for," Trout added.

"That's what I said," Snatcher snapped. "Everything I worked for."

"Erh, you said 'I' again," Trout mumbled.

"Oh, it's all the same thing, Trout," objected Pickles.

"You know, I don't think it is," Trout countered.

"Stop your quibbling!" Snatcher said. "We have work to do."

"But they got away," Trout pointed out. "It's over."

From the other side of the manhole, Eggs could practically feel Snatcher glaring at Trout.

"Over?" he said. "*Over?* Utter nonsense. It ain't *ever* over till the fat lady sings. It is time, gentlemen, to call Madame Frou Frou."

"Call her?" Pickles asked. "But I thought she was really just something you…Oh, I see. Quite right. Very clever, boss!"

"Yes, but who is calling her—we, or I?" pressed Trout.

Eggs heard the sound of muttering, and a brief scuffle, and the unmistakable sound of a boot connecting very hard with a Red Hat's behind.

Chapter 11

Winnie did not stop screaming from the moment she slid down the Boxtroll chute, onto the conveyor belt, and into the pile of sleeping Boxtrolls.

Their slumber rudely interrupted, the Boxtrolls began to stir. All around her, boxes suddenly sprouted arms and legs and heads. Winnie opened her mouth and began to scream again.

"They're everywhere! The planet is *seething* with Boxtrolls!" she shrieked.

She scrambled backward, away from the pile, until her back collided with the cavern wall. Then she flung both hands up in front of her face.

"No, get away! Stay away from me! Don't come any closer! Someone help me! Wealthy girl in danger!"

Winnie buried her face in her hands, stifling a sob.

"I expect my toes will make the prettiest necklace any of you have ever seen," she said with a sniff. Then she pulled herself together, clasped her hands in front of her, and bravely prepared to meet her maker.

But no one was paying the slightest bit of attention to her. All the Boxtrolls were gathered around Eggs.

"I'm telling you, I saw them," Eggs said. "It's not just me and Fish who made it—they're *all* alive! All of them!"

The Boxtrolls were gurgling with delight and amazement, drumming their claws on their boxes and nudging each other.

"What are they doing?" Winnie asked. "What's going on?"

"I saw them with my own eyes," Eggs promised them. "Books, Sparky, Knickers, Oil Can—I'm telling you, they're all alive!"

"*Bloob beskka?*" chortled a small, sweet-looking Boxtroll in a candy box.

"The Red Hats are keeping them in a pit in a big old factory on Curd's Way," Eggs said. "They're forcing them to work. I think they're making them build something."

Winnie was beginning to feel less in fear for her own life and more personally affronted that no one was interested in the magnificent necklace her toes would make.

"What's wrong with them?" she asked Eggs, looking mildly outraged. "Why aren't they ripping out our eyeballs and slurping our intestines like noodles?"

On hearing Winnie's question, several Boxtrolls disappeared into their boxes. Winnie didn't notice.

"Where are the rivers of blood and mountains of bones? *I was promised mountains of bones!*"

A chorus of frightened squeaks of various pitches came from the Boxtrolls, who were now all hiding in their boxes.

"I already told you, we don't eat people!" Eggs said, shaking his head. "We only eat bugs. Look—you scared them!"

Winnie took a few steps forward.

"Okay, why do you keep saying 'we' when you talk about the Boxtrolls? You're not one of them—you're a boy!"

A bad feeling began to spread in Eggs's stomach, like he'd swallowed a bug that wasn't quite dead.

"Of course I'm one of them. Of course I'm a Boxtroll. I'm Eggs! Don't you see my box?"

He pointed down, then stopped. He had forgotten he was in disguise. Relief swept over him. *That's* what the problem was—she was just confused by his Sabatino outfit.

"I mean, I'm not wearing my box right now because I had to put on a disguise to go into Cheesebridge. But I have one. I can disappear into my box just like any of them."

Eggs pointed at what now looked to be a simple stack of inanimate boxes.

"Really? Prove it. Get your box and disappear into it," Winnie said.

Eggs pictured his tattered, grimy box and remembered how lately it had gotten so small, he could barely get it over his head.

"It's, uh, at the tailor's, getting adjusted," Eggs said. "I'm unusually long-boned."

"Uh-huh," Winnie said, looking skeptical. "And what about your speech? You don't talk anything like them."

"I have a … It's a speech impediment," Eggs snapped. "Nice of you to bring it up.…Way to make a Boxtroll feel sensitive."

"Your ears aren't pointy," Winnie persisted.

The bad feeling in Eggs's stomach came back. It was true; no Boxtroll had ears like his.

"I slept on them funny," Eggs mumbled.

"Oh, for goodness' sake," Winnie exclaimed. "Okay, give me your hand."

Eggs felt he'd rather be trapped in a small lifeboat with Madame Frou Frou than show Winnie his undersized, oddly shaped, clawless hands. He tried to hide them behind his back.

Winnie lunged forward and grabbed one. Then she pulled him toward Fish, who had popped back out of his box. Summoning all her courage, Winnie grabbed Fish's ham-sized hand, too. Then she held the two together.

"Do these look alike to you?" Winnie asked.

"I don't know," Eggs said, but at the same time, Fish sadly shook his head.

Winnie dropped Fish's hand and discreetly wiped her own hand off on her skirt before pressing it against Eggs's.

"Now look at my hand. Do our hands look alike?"

Fish nodded.

"I rest my case," Winnie declared. "You are not a Boxtroll, Eggs. You are not one of them. You are one of us. You're a *boy*, Eggs."

Eggs's mouth hung open. He pulled his hand away and stared at Fish.

"Fish?" Eggs asked. "Tell her it's not true. I'm a Boxtroll. Fish, I'm a Boxtroll, right?"

Fish looked down at the ground and shook his head.

Eggs was positively dumbstruck. Yesterday he thought his world was coming to an end. Today he found out it wasn't even his world to begin with.

"See?" Winnie asked. "Now tell him the rest of the truth, Fish. Tell him you stole him when he was a baby."

"Glick bluddnt mwus!" Fish exclaimed indignantly. *"Ble mun goolibbendengluss!"*

Fish's voice sounded to Eggs like it was coming from far, far away. But automatically, he translated.

"He says...he says they didn't steal me. He says I was given...entrusted...to him...." Eggs whispered.

"Exactly what I—wait, what?"

Eggs looked at Winnie, then at Fish.

"Fish? Is this all true? Who gave me to you?"

Fish sighed and burbled, pointing at some stacks of

fabric tied up and resting near the waterwheel.

"He says we should sit down and get comfortable," Eggs told Winnie. "He says it's a long story."

It *was* a long story, especially for Winnie, because she first had to listen to Fish gurgle, then wait while Eggs asked questions and looked disbelieving or angry or sad or confused, then finally translated for her. Winnie worked very hard to keep the details straight, because she knew they were of Great Historical Import.

The child had disappeared exactly ten years ago and was the son of a kindly inventor whom Fish was somehow friends with. In fact, according to what Fish was saying, all the Boxtrolls knew and liked the baby's father, and they often worked on gadgets together. The man didn't even call them Boxtrolls; he called them "builders," and they helped each other with all kinds of inventions. In fact, they were all extremely fond of one another.

Winnie tried not to look skeptical. She had never heard of any human who was friends with Boxtrolls. Why would this information be kept secret? Then again, Eggs himself was clearly a Boxtroll friend, and he was clearly human. Winnie kept her mind open and continued to listen.

One night the man was working late, with only one Boxtroll to keep him company.

"Glendalebun giggy bang!" Fish said. *"Blabglan wubame blin."*

"There was a bang, and the door burst open, and men burst into his house," Eggs translated.

Fish added some more babbling details.

"One man had a bat, one had a net, and one hollered and yelled and ordered the man around," Eggs said. "They all wore red hats."

"Gristle, Pickles, and Snatcher," Winnie said, and Eggs nodded his agreement.

Fish jabbered excitedly as Eggs's expression grew increasingly horrified.

"They ordered the man to make something bad, a weapon maybe, and he refused to do it," Eggs explained. "When he refused, Snatcher told him they were going to take him away. When he thought they weren't looking, the man put his baby in the Boxtroll's box and said, 'Whatever happens, keep him safe.' And then…"

Eggs stopped. He had tears in his eyes. Fish had tears in his big yellow eyes, too. Fish put a comforting claw on Eggs's shoulder.

"...then there was a terrible loud noise, and a *thud*. And when the Boxtroll peeked to see what had happened, he saw the man lying on the floor, dead."

Winnie gasped. Snatcher had killed a poor innocent man for refusing to make an evil invention?

"Blubenn guweggs dubarted bly!" Fish said, weeping.

"And then the baby started to cry," Eggs said grimly.

Fish strung a long, rapid-fire line of gurgles together, punctuated by little sobs.

"Following the sound of the baby, the Red Hats discovered the Boxtroll. When Snatcher saw the Boxtroll, he ordered his men to capture it. But the Boxtroll ran off with the baby. And he didn't stop running until he got to the underground cave where he lived, and could make sure the baby was safe. It was his human friend's last request before he was killed, and the Boxtroll vowed to carry it out."

Now Winnie was crying, too.

"The baby lived among the Boxtrolls, and was loved and cared for by all of them, and was raised as one of their own," Eggs said.

Fish nodded.

"I was that baby," Eggs said.

Fish nodded.

"The man that Snatcher killed was my father," Eggs said again, his voice trembling.

Fish nodded.

"And you…" he said to Fish, "you were with my father that night. You were the Boxtroll he entrusted me to. You were the one he asked to keep me safe."

His head hanging so low it almost touched the ground, Fish nodded one last time.

"All these years you've taken care of me, even though I'm human. Even though humans have been hunting the Boxtrolls like vermin."

Fish's head snapped up.

"Bleemuddindat. Glubearbox, glubarrboxtroll. Goobammlee."

Eggs wiped his eyes.

"He says it doesn't matter. I wear a box, so I'm a Boxtroll. I'm family," Eggs whispered.

He stumbled forward and enveloped Fish in a clumsy hug. Fish hugged him back, sniffling and reaching one clawed hand up to gently stroke Eggs's head.

Winnie watched, utterly flabbergasted. She felt like her head was spinning. Everything she'd been told, everything she had ever been raised to believe her entire life, was a lie. She burst into tears, startling Fish and Eggs out of their hug.

"All these years we've been taught to hate you!" she sobbed. "We've been taught to cheer on the Red Hats who hunt you—the same ones who killed your father! This is all their doing! They even used you, Eggs, to make us afraid of the Boxtrolls."

"Used me?" Eggs asked. "How?"

"I told you back in the factory. Don't you remember?" Winnie asked. "Haven't you put it all together? The Red Hats used the story of the abduction and murder of the Trubshaw baby to scare Cheesebridge. But they made it up; it's all a lie. The only killers that night were Red Hats. Don't you see, Eggs? It's you. The little baby Fish hid in his box.

"You are the Trubshaw baby."

Chapter 12

When Fish finally returned Winnie to Eggs's nook after an exhaustive tour of the cave and its every contraption, Winnie was exhausted.

I could use a nap, she thought. She looked over at Eggs, who was sitting on an old rolled-up rug.

He's barely said anything except to translate for Fish, Winnie thought. *And he looks so sad. Poor kid.*

"Hey, so where's this Music Machine you mentioned?" Winnie asked.

Eggs's face brightened, but only a little. He stood up and walked over to it.

"This is it," he said. "You can do different stuff with it—program it, play some instruments on it. It even plays old records."

"And you and Fish built it all by yourselves?" Winnie asked, truly impressed.

Eggs nodded.

"Golly. Boxtrolls are amazing," Winnie said. She

bent down and picked up an old record lying on the floor.

"Oh, wow, I had this record, too!" Winnie exclaimed. "This exact one! I left it by the window one night and the next morning it was gone. I was sooooo irritated. I guess it must have fallen out or...hey! I think this *is* my record!"

Eggs looked up at her, but he didn't seem to be listening.

"What do fathers do?" Eggs asked.

Winnie put the record down and sat on the rolled-up rug. She patted a spot next to her, and Eggs sat down.

"That song from today," Eggs said. "That the big ugly lady sang on the outside stage. It said something about the Trubshaw baby's father searching for him."

Winnie nodded thoughtfully.

"Well, a father is the one who raises you, I guess. Looks after you, feeds you, keeps you safe. Loves you."

"Like Fish," Eggs suggested.

"Well, kind of. I mean, Fish did those things for you, just like your father asked. So he's kind of acted like a father to you. But a real father...you know, they always listen to you and never get mad, and they guide you when you can't figure out what to do. They spend time with you because they want to, instead of just buying you junk to keep you quiet. And they're always there for you, even when you're scared or lonely or you hear a strange noise outside....A father is never too busy to talk to you and make you feel safe, and..."

Winnie's voice trailed off. A lump rose in her throat.

"Hey, wait, though," Eggs said. "You have a father. So we could go to him for help!"

"What?" Winnie exclaimed. "Oh, no, no...sorry. I gave you the wrong idea. I mean, I do have a father, but he's not...like other fathers. You can't imagine what he's like."

"But he's the only father we have right now," Eggs said. "Winnie, you have to try. *Please.* Everyone I love is being held prisoner in that factory."

Winnie nodded.

"I know. And Snatcher plans to kill every one of them."

"What?" cried Eggs, springing to his feet.

"Oh, I'm sorry, Eggs! I shouldn't have just blurted that out, but honestly, I just put it all together. I heard

Snatcher say that to my father last night. He's such a deluded slimeball, he somehow thinks that killing all the Boxtrolls will make Father grateful enough to promote him to a White Hat."

"Then you *have* to help," Eggs said.

"Okay, listen," Winnie told Eggs, grasping his arm. "If I agree to try, you have to promise me that you will do exactly as I say."

"Of course! I promise!" Eggs exclaimed.

"All right. Well, the first thing we need is a makeover."

"A makeover?" asked Eggs.

"That's right," Winnie said. "Head to toe. Right now you are a walking hygiene and fashion disaster. Cowboy up, Eggs. We've got to change you into a real boy."

Eggs tried to project his consciousness elsewhere over the next few hours, as he was bathed, scrubbed, buffed, polished, sheared, coiffed, and measured. As Winnie worked on him, she called out requests to the Boxtrolls, who scampered off and returned with assorted items and fabrics.

Now Eggs was facing the indignity of standing in a

clean pair of underwear with his arms out in a T as Winnie held up various swatches of fabric beneath his chin.

"No, absolutely not. This is a *terrible* color for you," she said. "Next?"

A small Boxtroll darted forward and held up some cloth. Winnie gasped and clutched the string of pearls around her neck.

"Velour?" she asked. "For formal evening wear? Were you raised in a barn?"

The Boxtroll ran away, and another one stepped forward with an armful of something fluffy and shiny.

Winnie reached for it, ran her hands over it, and exclaimed in delight, "Silk chiffon! Oh, we can definitely use this!" She leaned down close to the Boxtroll who had brought it. "Can you find more like this? Silk. Siilllllk. Can you find more? Chiffon, and satin will do nicely, too. Okay? Yes? *Capisce?* What, am I speaking another language?"

Eggs sighed and turned to the group of observing Boxtrolls.

"She wants shinies. Shinies to wear like boxes," he explained.

The Boxtrolls instantly took off in eight different directions.

"Excellent," Winnie said. "While they're doing that, try on these pants I made you for size."

It took a little awkward explaining and pantomiming for Eggs to grasp the concept of putting on a pair of pants, one leg at a time. Thankfully, once he was in them, he seemed to have no trouble with the zipper and the button.

"Very nice," Winnie said. "They fit perfectly. How do they feel?"

Eggs squirmed and tugged on the waistband and repeatedly kicked out his right foot like he was trying to shake a snake off his leg.

"They feel awful," he complained. "They are tight around my tummy and they tickle my ankles."

"They're supposed to," Winnie said. "We must suffer for beauty. Everyone knows that."

I don't know it, Eggs thought, but he decided to keep the sentiment to himself.

The same Boxtroll who had found the silk chiffon returned with a roll of shimmering blue material.

"Oh, well done," said Winnie. "That's absolutely the right thing."

The Boxtroll squirmed and fidgeted and looked extra pleased, until the one standing next to him smacked him with a roll of tin foil.

"I'm just going to need to do a bit more sewing," Winnie said. "Sit down, Eggs. We'll be done before too much longer."

Eggs sat down, then almost immediately stood up again. He tried stretching the pants every which way, then finally gave up and lay down flat on his back.

Winnie glanced at him occasionally as she sewed.

"I'm really sorry about your father," she said quietly. "You must miss him very much."

Eggs shrugged, which is difficult to do properly while lying down.

"Until today, I didn't even remember him," he said. "I thought I was born here. I thought I was a Boxtroll. The poor guy died trying to save me, and I didn't even remember he existed. Shows you how much his fatherly love was worth—I obviously didn't love him."

Winnie temporarily dropped her sewing.

"It's worth more than anything in the world, Eggs," Winnie cried. "And don't you ever forget it. And I'll tell you something else. Any baby who has a father so loving, a father who would do anything, even die, to protect his child—any baby who is loved *that* much most definitely loves his father right back. You might not remember it, Eggs, but I promise you that you loved your father every bit as much as he loved you, and he knew it. And you should be happy about that, because not everyone has it. Some people don't."

Winnie rubbed her eyes, bowed her head, and picked up her sewing again.

"Some people like who?" Eggs asked, propping himself into a sitting position.

"Some people like some people," Winnie said. "You really never know. Now, you've got to stop chattering, Eggs, or I'm never going to get this finished."

Egg obediently stopped talking. When Winnie told him to stand or hold his arm out or put his hands on his hips, he did it without comment.

She must be allergic to that blue fabric, Eggs thought. *Her eyes are all red and runny.*

Finally, Winnie stood up.

"Here," she said. "Put this jacket on."

Eggs held it up over his head like it was an umbrella and swatted at it with his other hand.

"Here, give it," Winnie said with a sigh. "Same

idea as pants: Slide in one arm, then the other. The opening goes in the back. If the opening is in the front, that means you put the wrong arm in the wrong sleeve."

"But if I put the wrong arm in the wrong sleeve, wouldn't that make it the right sleeve?" Eggs asked.

"Stop talking and let me look at you," Winnie commanded.

She took a few steps back and stared at Eggs.

He looked clean and shiny and polished and civilized. With one glaring exception.

Winnie groaned.

"Your feet!" she cried. "What the dickens are we going to do about those? Those teddy bear sneakers are revolting. I may be a decent seamstress, but I can't make a pair of fancy dress shoes!"

Shoe waddled up to Winnie and gurgled.

"I'm sorry, what? Could you speak up a little?" Winnie asked.

Shoe reached into his box and pulled out a pair of shiny black shoes.

"Ooh, yes, those might work," Winnie said hopefully. "Can you get yourself into these, Eggs?"

Eggs looked suspiciously at the narrow, shiny

shoes, shook his head, sat down, and stuck his feet in the air. He kicked off the old sneakers, and after a bit of pushing and tugging and a number of squeals, the new shoes were on and neatly laced up.

Winnie held out her hand and pulled Eggs to a standing position. She gave him a long, thorough look, then nodded.

"Well, it's…it's something, all right. You know, you look like an actual boy now," she said.

"An actual boy," Eggs repeated quietly.

The Boxtrolls, who had been inching closer and closer to get a better view, all began beating their boxes and emitting little gurgling cheers of approval. Eggs took a deep bow and added a little curly flourish with one hand.

"Okay, okay, don't bury yourself in the part," Winnie grumbled. "Your makeover took a lot longer than I thought. If I'm going to get to my father in time, we need to get going right now. Okay, Eggs?"

"Okay!" Eggs agreed. "I'm ready to go save the Boxtrolls, and nothing in this world or any other is going to stop me!"

He took one step forward, caught the toe of the

dress shoe on a bump in the floor, and went sprawling
face-first in the dirt.

Winnie shook her head in exasperation.

"You're going to have to do a little better than that,"
she told him.

Eggs sat up and brushed himself off, grinning.

"Don't worry," he told her. "I will."

Chapter 13

By the time Eggs and Winnie reached Market Square, it was dark outside. The Cheese Guild was lit up like a birthday cake. Light poured from every window, and the whole building seemed to shimmer and glisten against the gloomy backdrop of night.

"Wow, so shiny," Eggs remarked, dazzled by the light. He walked quickly across the square, Winnie trailing behind him. She couldn't help but notice he walked more like an ape than a boy. Just as he reached the Cheese Guild steps, he wiped his nose on his sleeve and reached behind and scratched his bottom.

"Eggs!" Winnie hissed.

He turned and gave her a wide-eyed, innocent look.

"You have to walk more slowly and elegantly, like a dancer. You never wipe your nose or your mouth or anything with your sleeve or any other part of your clothing, or your hand. And never scratch your...

backside in public. Or your front side. All those things are extremely rude!"

Eggs looked genuinely confounded.

"Why?" he asked.

Winnie groaned. She'd spent so much time on his appearance, she had forgotten about his behavior. She grabbed his arms and pulled him off the steps and away from the light of the big front door.

"Okay, look. For this to work, there are a few things you're going to need to know. First, when you meet someone, you have to look them in the eye and then shake hands."

"Hello," Eggs said, opening his eyes so wide they bulged and raising both hands in the air and shaking them around.

"Stop kidding around," Winnie said.

"What? That wasn't right?" Eggs asked.

Oh, brother, Winnie thought. *What have I gotten myself into?*

"Here," she said, taking his right hand in hers.

"Hello, it's a pleasure to meet you," she said in a crisp, snooty accent while simultaneously pumping their clasped hands up and down. "Say it just like that.

Even if you're *not* pleased to meet them. As for everything else..."

Eggs's face looked strained, and he frowned with concentration.

"Oh, forget it," Winnie said. "Just remember that, and to stand up straight, shoulders back, chin up. Got it?"

"I think so," Eggs said. He went rigid, like he'd received a mild electrical shock.

"Oh...just stick close to me, all right?" Winnie said. "Come on. Let's get inside."

They climbed the steps and Winnie pushed open the huge front door. Immediately, a wave of sound swept over them, many voices talking and laughing at the same time. The entrance hall was filled with men and women dressed in luxurious suits and gowns and opulent furs and jewels. Eggs had never seen so many shinies in one place in his life.

"Where is your father?" he asked.

Winnie scanned the room anxiously.

"I don't know," she said. "He's usually somewhere making a speech about cheese."

A tall, oddly stick-thin woman with upswept hair

and an abundance of enormous jewelry caught sight of Winnie and gave a half wave with two fingers.

"Winifred," she called. "Darling. Where have you been? We're already on the appetizers."

Eggs thought the poor lady must have had something wrong with her mouth, because when she talked, it sounded like her teeth were all stuck together, uppers clamped onto lowers.

"Hello, Mommy dearest," Winnie said.

"You must...Oh," Winnie's mother said, drawing back slightly and clutching her necklace. "Who is... this?"

"Eggs," said Eggs.

"Bert," Winnie continued quickly. "This is Eggsbert. Eggsbert Benedict. A perfectly normal name."

"Eggsbert," murmured Winnie's mother, staring at a passing waiter. "I do love those old-timey names from the Bible."

Eggs grabbed the woman's hand and pumped it so hard that one of her bracelets flew off and landed on the floor with a clatter.

"It's a pleasure to meet you, Mommy dearest, even if it isn't," Eggs said with great confidence.

Winnie winced, and her mother's eyebrows shot up.

"You don't shake a lady's hand, only a gentleman's...." Winnie whispered.

"Winifred!" her mother interrupted. "What in the world are you wearing? You should have changed into your after-lunch, early-evening Tuesday dress. Come along with me this instant."

As Winnie's mother began to take her away, Winnie hissed at Eggs, "Try to fit in! When in doubt, say nothing! I'll be right back...."

Eggs did his best, but everything about the scene was so unnerving. There were so many Cheese Bits, all of them draped in layer upon layer of shinies. Instead of a Music Machine, they had people playing instruments, and some of the Cheese Bits were dancing. Eggs had to duck and sidestep to avoid being slammed into. He really did try to remember everything Winnie had taught him, but when he met another lady, he could only remember that shaking her hand was *wrong*, and he got confused and ended up licking her hand instead, which caused a small scene from which he hastily retreated.

Maybe I should go eat something, Eggs thought. *I might not have to talk to anyone if I do that.*

There was a long table laden with food, but none of

it looked particularly appetizing, until Eggs caught sight of a single ladybug crawling up a stem in a flower arrangement. Was it rude to take the last bug? But he was so hungry....

Eggs reached out, grabbed the ladybug, and popped it into his mouth.

He heard a gasp and looked up to see Winnie's mother staring at him, evidently aghast.

I did something rude, Eggs guessed. He stared around at the other guests, who were all taking dainty bites of various things on crackers.

Oh, the crackers!

Gingerly, he spat the ladybug into his hand, picked up a cracker, placed the ladybug on top of it, and popped the whole thing back in his mouth.

Winnie's mother looked like she was about to faint dead away.

But the bug had awakened Eggs's appetite. He moved down the table, shoving various things into his mouth, two and three at a time. When he paused to make another selection, Eggs noticed a number of Cheese Bits were looking at him strangely.

Now what? he wondered.

Then he noticed that all the Cheese Bits who were

eating things from that end of the table were using little forks. Ah, okay. Eggs could do that.

He picked up a fork, spat his partially chewed-up cheese ball into his hand, scooped it up with the fork, and popped it back into his mouth.

I'm really adapting to these strange customs fast! Eggs thought with pride.

"Ladies and gentlemen, your attention, please!"

"Quiet, everyone. Lord Portley-Rind is speaking!" someone bellowed.

Eggs turned and saw the large Cheese Bit with the red beard he'd seen at the Trubshaw baby memorial procession.

"Welcome, distinguished notables and muckety-mucks," the man continued. "As you know, we originally planned this gala to celebrate the successful fund-raising efforts for a new children's hospital. But after some discussion, my fellow White Hats and I decided the money would be much better spent on something else. Without further ado, I present...*the Party Havarti*!"

Lord Portley-Rind stepped aside, revealing an enormous rounded shape covered by a sheet. With a great flourish, he whipped off the sheet, revealing a massive wheel of cheese. The assembled Cheese Bits went wild, gasping and clutching one another and cheering with all their might.

"What in the world is the point of that?" Eggs wondered aloud.

"Oh, *nephew*!" a suspiciously shrill voice called from nearby. "There you are, *mon petit fromage!*"

People turned around and stared at Eggs.

Is that person talking to me? he wondered, looking around.

A mountain of a woman was barreling toward him, dressed in layers and layers of ruffles and shinies, and so heavily made up, she looked a little alarming. She reached forward and grabbed Eggs's arm tightly with a heavily bejeweled hand, plucking a piece of cheese from the table with her other hand and popping it into her mouth.

"Zees parties are so confusing, no? Let Madame Frou Frou help."

Frou Frou! The woman from the Trubshaw play. She looked much, much scarier close up.

"Uh, pleased to meet you," Eggs said.

Madame Frou Frou beamed and extended her large, hairy hand.

None of the other Cheese Bit ladies have hair on their hands, Eggs thought. *Or knuckles that enormous. And painting those lips red is a big mistake—it just calls attention to them.*

And was Eggs simply disoriented by the bright lights and the crowd, or were Madame Frou Frou's fingers growing fatter before his very eyes?

Eggs looked up at Madame Frou Frou and noticed that several distinct red blotches had appeared on her face. Just like the blotches that Red Hat got after eating cheese…and *his* hands had swollen up, too!

"You're no lady—you're Snatcher!" Eggs cried.

The fake smile was replaced by a snarl, and Snatcher slapped his grotesque, still-swelling hand over Eggs's mouth.

"Don't make a scene, kid," he said, dropping the falsetto voice altogether. He yanked Eggs hard by the arm and dragged him into a small room filled with coats. He kicked the door shut, then grabbed Eggs by both shoulders.

"Come to snitch on old Snatcher, have you?" he hissed, releasing a cloud of truly hideous breath in Eggs's face. "Do you really think a highfalutin fellow like Portley-Rind and his fancy ilk will help a nobody like *you*? In this town, if you want help, you've got to help yourself. That's what a *real* man does!"

With his lipstick and blue eye shadow and dangly clip-on earrings, Snatcher didn't look all that much like a man to Eggs.

"You're nothing but a lying monster," Eggs snapped. "When I tell Winnie's father the truth about you, he'll put a stop to you and your lies *for good*."

Snatcher began rifling through the hanging coats as if he was looking for something, but still hung on to Eggs with his free hand to prevent him from escaping.

"Tomorrow, I'll be the most respected man in Cheesebridge," Snatcher growled. "They'll have *no* choice but to give me a white hat. They'll parade me into the Tasting Room on their shoulders. I'll finally be accepted for who I really am!"

Snatcher found a long scarf in one of the coat pockets. He wound it tightly around Eggs's wrists.

"And if you think I'm going to let some little Boxtroll-loving sewer rat get in my way, you're out of your mind," Snatcher said, moving to wrap the rest of the scarf around Eggs's neck.

Eggs only had time to think, *He's going to kill me.* But suddenly the door flew open and someone came in.

"Madame Frou Frou, *there* you are, you Cracker-slovakian minx. You promised me a dance!"

"I did?" Snatcher asked, then quickly switched to his Madame Frou Frou voice.

"Of course I did, Lord Langsdale!"

Langsdale gave Snatcher a reptilian grin.

"Well, I simply can't wait a moment longer, madame," Langsdale said, taking hold of Snatcher's arm and pulling firmly.

"Oh, watch those hands, now, Langsdale," Snatcher squeaked in his Frou Frou voice.

And then Eggs was alone in the closet.

"Phew," he mumbled. "That was close."

Eggs emerged cautiously from the closet. Snatcher was nowhere to be seen, and Lord Portley-Rind was still up on the steps, stroking the massive wheel of cheese like it was a pony. But there was a sea of people between Eggs and the stairs. How was he ever going to get to Lord Portley-Rind?

There had to be a way.

And the life of every Boxtroll in the Red Hat factory depended on Eggs's figuring out what it was.

Chapter 14

E ggs! There you are!"

Eggs almost shouted with relief when he saw Winnie bearing down on him.

"We've got to get to your father," Eggs said urgently.

Winnie glanced at the room thick with people.

"No problem," she said. "We'll dance through."

"We'll what?" asked Eggs.

"Just follow my lead," Winnie said. "It's a waltz— easiest dance there is. Just step in threes—one-two-three, one-two-three, one-two-three—so you make a box."

"But you took my box," Eggs objected.

"A box shape. With your steps. One-two-three, one-two-three."

Suddenly, they were twirling and spinning around the room. Eggs laughed out loud. He'd never seen dancing like this before—Boxtroll dancing was completely different. But he had to admit to himself it was fun!

In the midst of a twirl, Eggs caught a glimpse of Snatcher's enraged face, and all thoughts of fun left his mind.

"Snatcher's here," he told Winnie.

"What? Where?"

"Dancing with that Langsdale guy," he told her.

Winnie did a double take, then looked horrified.

"We've got to—" she began, but she was drowned out by the booming voice of her father.

"Let's keep it exciting, everyone!" he called. "Everyone change partners *now*!"

Eggs just had time to see Winnie mouth *sorry* before he was whisked away by a chubby woman who smelled so strongly of perfume that Eggs felt his eyes burning.

"That's the way! Enjoy it while you can, people—in two more minutes, everyone will change partners again!" Lord Portley-Rind called, looking excessively pleased with himself.

Eggs saw to his horror that Snatcher was forcing his partner closer and closer to Eggs.

Snatcher's going to try to dance with me next, Eggs thought. It was a horrifying thought for an endless number of reasons.

"And...*change*!" Lord Portley-Rind called.

"Eggs, look out!" Winnie barked, stomping on her dance partner's foot so she could break free.

Snatcher lunged for Eggs. Quickly, Eggs dropped to the floor. Camouflaged by the sea of billowing skirts, he scrambled away on his hands and knees, heading for the stairs. He had a clear shot at Lord Portley-Rind now.

Lord Portley-Rind was so consumed by stroking, smelling, and admiring the massive cheese wheel that he did not even notice Eggs clambering toward him. Eggs was practically at Lord Portley-Rind's feet when someone grabbed his leg hard.

"Let me *go*!!" Eggs bellowed, and Lord Portley-Rind finally noticed him.

"What the devil..." the large red-haired man began.

Eggs bent almost in half and sank his teeth into Snatcher's hand, biting down as hard as he could. Snatcher let out a deafening howl and maneuvered himself between an angry Eggs and an astonished Lord Portley-Rind.

"My lord, I have to warn you that—" Snatcher began, and Eggs dove at him, figuring a body tackle might shut him up.

But Snatcher ducked, and Eggs went sailing over

him, colliding violently with the enormous wheel of cheese. The wheel teetered back and forth precariously, then rocked clear off the small pedestal holding it.

"NOOOOOOOOOOOOOOOO!" Lord Portley-Rind screamed as the cheese began half rolling, half bouncing down the staircase.

It was a sight both magnificent and horrifying. The crowd parted like the Red Sea as the colossal wheel bounced on the floor and continued to roll, gaining speed and momentum as it went.

There was nothing anyone could do. In a matter of seconds, the cheese had rolled out the front door, which happened to be standing open, and bounced regally down the steps.

The room fell deathly quiet. Through the open door, the cheese could still be seen, rolling across Market Square.

An excessively short bald man near the stairs remarked, "Wow. Sure hope it stops before it reaches the—"

A huge splash sounded in the distance.

"...river," the man finished quietly.

Lord Portley-Rind was absolutely frozen with shock. Eggs felt a hand gently touch his shoulder.

"Well, at least you got his attention," Winnie said with a rueful smile.

Everyone in the room, Lord Portley-Rind included, was now staring at Eggs.

"WHAT...HAVE...YOU...DONE?" he bellowed, his face bright red with rage.

Eggs stood up. Straight. Shoulders back. Chin up.

"Mr....uh, Lord Winnie's dad, and all you people of Cheesebridge, Archibald Snatcher has been lying and deceiving every single one of you!" Eggs declared. "He has told you that Boxtrolls are monsters, that they steal and eat children, but that isn't true! Boxtrolls have never hurt anyone. I know that, because I've spent almost my entire life with them. They are my family. And I...*I am the Trubshaw baby!*"

Lord Portley-Rind was thunderstruck. He scratched his head, squinted as if in deep thought, then opened his mouth. After a moment, he closed it again. He turned and stared very hard at the place where the Party Havarti had been just moments earlier. He extended one foot in its long, pointy shoe and slid it around on the step, as if he expected it to connect with the Party Havarti, which would be found to be not missing, but simply rendered temporarily invisible. His foot found nothing. He turned and fixed Eggs with a dark look.

"Do you," he said, pointing at Eggs, "have any idea…how much that cheese *cost*?"

"I said I am the Trub—what?"

Eggs must have misunderstood Lord Portley-Rind. Surely the man wasn't simply going to ignore the bombshell Eggs had just dropped.

"We might as well have built that silly children's hospital now," Lord Portley-Rind said, shaking his head.

"Father!" exclaimed Winnie. "Did you hear a word he just said?"

"Do you know how long it is going to take my men to pull that cheese out of the river?" Lord Portley-Rind barked. "I don't know how they're going to do it without scarring the rind."

"If you won't listen to me, sir, ask Snatcher yourself! He's right there. Yeah, that's right—your beloved Madame Frou Frou is actually Snatcher in disguise. He's been making complete idiots of you all!" Eggs cried.

Everyone began to laugh.

"Stop laughing!" Winnie yelled. "He's telling the

truth. Eggs, *show* them," she said, yanking on her hair.

Eggs immediately understood. Before Snatcher had a chance to back away, Eggs plucked the wig right off his head.

The crowd fell silent, their expressions changing.

"Oh, my," Snatcher said. "You have me. I am...you see...the truth is, I am...*not* really a redhead."

"This is an outrage!" shouted someone.

"The very thought!" yelled another.

"I always knew there was something not quite right about Frou Frou!" exclaimed a woman.

Lord Portley-Rind's dark look had changed to a livid stare.

"You have disrupted my celebration and insulted the guest of honor! Who are you?" he demanded.

"I'm...I'm a boy," Eggs said.

"And how did you get into this building, boy?" Lord Portley-Rind asked.

"He came with me," Winnie said, folding her arms and lifting her chin defiantly. "He's my friend, and everything he's told you is *true*."

"ENOUGH!" Lord Portley-Rind hollered. "You, boy. I never want to see you again. Do you understand? Leave my house. *Now!*"

Eggs was stunned. Winnie was standing with her head hanging.

This was it? Everything they had gone through, just to be ignored and humiliated? Everyone there had heard Eggs say he was the Trubshaw baby they all pretended to care about so much. But the truth was, they *didn't* care. They were only interested in their things, and their clothes, and their...their cheese!

Eggs turned and walked silently down the steps.

"Toodle-loo!" sang Snatcher, waving.

The crowd drew back as Eggs passed. No one spoke to him, but everyone stared. He walked out the front door and down the steps.

Moments later, the music started again.

On the far side of Market Square, Eggs struggled to dislodge a manhole cover. He was so exhausted and demoralized, he could scarcely manage it. He sat back on his haunches for a moment, hearing the sound of footsteps running toward him.

"Eggs! Eggs!" Winnie called.

Eggs looked up at Winnie wearily. "You said fathers *helped*. You said they took care of their children," he said bitterly.

"They're supposed to," Winnie replied.

Eggs gave the manhole cover a yank, and this time it slid free.

"People Aboveground are just mean and selfish. They're monsters," he said, beginning to climb into the manhole.

"Not all of them are," Winnie said. "You're not."

Eggs gave her a sad look.

"Well, I don't want to be a boy anymore. I'm going back underground. It was...a pleasure to meet you, Winnie," Eggs told her.

"Oh, Eggs..." Winnie said, tears welling in her eyes.

"I really do mean that," he said. "But I need to go home now."

Winnie didn't try to stop him as he dropped out of sight.

Chapter 15

Eggs popped off the conveyor belt and onto the landing pillow. He ducked out of sight for a moment. He didn't want to tell them what had happened. He didn't want to admit he'd failed. He didn't want to see their eager faces just before they learned they were doomed. But he owed it to them. They were his family, his friends, his world. Even if they only had a short while left, they deserved to hear the truth from Eggs.

This is the worst day of my life, Eggs thought. Then he took a deep breath and strode into the center of the cave, waving. Immediately, he was surrounded by excited Boxtrolls. They babbled loudly and drummed on their boxes.

"No. *No!* Listen to me, all of you. It didn't work!" Eggs cried. "They're not going to help us. They don't care that Snatcher is going to destroy us all."

The Boxtrolls stopped drumming on their boxes and looked at one another.

"Snatcher is planning something—he's going to take the rest of us out. He thinks he'll get a white hat if he does. We have got to get out of here, okay? We have to leave the cavern!"

None of them moved.

"Did you hear what I just said?" asked Eggs. "We have to get out of here. Snatcher is coming for us. Maybe right this minute! We have to go *now*!"

Some of the Boxtrolls were backing away from Eggs and shaking their heads. Several others sat down on the ground.

"What are you *doing*? Get up! We have to go. Sparky, Knickers, you can't just hide."

But that is exactly what the Boxtrolls were doing, disappearing one after another into their boxes.

"Fish, help me!" Eggs pleaded.

Fish responded by handing Eggs his old box.

"No, I can't hide in there."

Fish persisted, pushing the box against Eggs's chest.

"No. *I am not a Boxtroll!*" Eggs shouted, smacking the box out of Fish's hands and kicking it away.

Fish immediately disappeared into his own box,

which was trembling along with him. Eggs knelt down next to him.

"Fish, I'm sorry. I didn't mean to scare you. Please come out. Please—we're running out of time!"

Suddenly, the entire cavern began to shudder and rumble as if it had been struck by an earthquake. Dust and debris rained down from the ceiling. The bulbs in the chandelier overhead began flickering. Then there was a popping sound, and the cavern went dark.

"It's too late," Eggs said quietly. "It's Snatcher. He's here."

The rumbling grew louder and louder. A crack appeared in the ceiling and quickly grew into a hole. Something sharp and shiny was eating away at the hole, making it bigger and bigger. Huge chunks of rock were crashing to the cavern floor. As Eggs watched in horror, a machine emerged, a massive drill capped by an enormous boxed cabin, the whole thing cobbled together with a series of gears and cables and canvas and metal.

So that's what Snatcher had the Boxtrolls building, Eggs thought.

The drill took several more bites out of the rock, and then the entire machine plunged through the hole and crashed onto the cavern floor. Boxtrolls scattered in every direction. As clouds of dust settled around the machine, two huge spotlights switched on. There was a whirring and grinding sound, then the box slowly raised itself on three metal legs, having deposited three Red Hats on the ground.

"Pickles, Trout, and Gristle," murmured Eggs. "But where is…"

There was a bang, and a hatch on top of the box flew open and a head appeared. It was Snatcher, still wearing his Frou Frou makeup. In the eerie light, his powdered face and crimson lipstick made him look like a clown who'd gone over to the dark side.

"How's *that* for an entrance?" Snatcher crowed.

"Dramatical!" said Pickles.

"The Bard himself would be impressed, boss," added Trout.

"We drilled through the earth!" Gristle announced.

"Time to earn me my white hat, lads!" Snatcher called.

The spotlights were moving, scanning the cave for fleeing Boxtrolls. The light seemed to paralyze them—instead of continuing to run, they curled up and hid in their boxes.

Gristle began rounding them up.

"*No!*" Eggs yelled. "What are you doing? Escape up the tube!!"

Eggs shoved several Boxtrolls closest to him toward the tube, but they remained huddled inside their boxes.

"My, my!" Snatcher called merrily. "What a surprise. Doesn't look like your little friends want to run away, does it?"

"Please," Eggs begged the Boxtrolls. "Just go to the tube!"

But as soon as he said it, a mechanical arm began to unfurl from the cabin of the drill machine. It extended itself to the Sucker-Upper, then promptly smashed it to bits. Eggs struggled to get the Boxtrolls out of the way.

Trout and Pickles were coming toward Eggs.

"A noble effort, Master Trubshaw," said Trout.

"But goodness always triumphs over evil in the end," Pickles added. "Which I'm pretty sure is *us*."

Eggs was still holding one of the cowering Boxtrolls, and Trout reached out and yanked the box from his hands. Pickles made a grab for Eggs, but the boy dove out of the way. As Trout added his catch to the pile of Boxtrolls he had corralled, another mechanical arm extended from the cabin and began to vacuum up the Boxtrolls.

"Don't hide! Stop hiding! You've got to fight back!" Eggs screamed.

Snatcher laughed.

"Ha! Boxtrolls fighting back? These gutless chickens? You know as well as I do, it just ain't in their nature!" Snatcher jeered.

"Stand up for yourselves! Fight!" Eggs pleaded.

But the Boxtrolls were all disappearing in front of his eyes, caught in nets, thrown in the pile, and sucked up into the giant machine. More mechanical arms unfurled, smashing everything in reach to bits. Within minutes the waterwheel was destroyed and the walls were tumbling down.

Eggs heard a whimper. It was Fish, huddled nearby in the remains of the garden. Eggs ran to him and clutched him.

"Stop it...please...." Eggs called.

The spotlights fell on Eggs, nearly blinding him.

"I told ya, kid, Boxtrolls never help themselves. That's why they'll always be losers," Snatcher called, adding a cheerful laugh.

Eggs reached into Fish's box and found his big hand. He squeezed it tightly. The giant vacuum was pivoting toward them. Eggs grabbed a giant cabbage from the ruined garden and hurled it into the nozzle, effectively blocking it.

Eggs grabbed Fish and began to back away, never noticing Gristle was pointing his net gun directly at them.

BLAM!

Everything went topsy-turvy. Eggs felt a tremendous pain in his head. He did not know if he was conscious or dreaming. He thought he heard Fish's voice, but it sounded so far away....

"Make sure to get the boy, too," Snatcher ordered. "I've got something special planned for him."

Rough hands reached into the net. Eggs felt himself being slung over someone's shoulder, but he couldn't move.

Then something began growling and hissing.

"Whoa!" Pickles cried. "Never seen one do that before! Careful of this one, fellas!"

"That is different behavior and makes me uneasy!" Gristle declared nervously.

"Got him!" Trout yelled.

Eggs tried to open his eyes. The last thing he saw was the drill spinning, continuing its destruction of the cavern as it made its ascent. Eggs caught a glimpse of his nook, with his precious Music Machine, collapsing in on itself.

Then, mercifully, everything went black and Eggs saw no more.

Chapter 16

When Eggs awakened, he found himself in a cage that was suspended from the ceiling of the old Red Hat factory. Nearby, another cage hung, slightly higher than his own. Eggs rubbed his eyes and peered down. The Red Hats were stacking all the captured Boxtrolls into neat piles under some sort of contraption. Eggs realized what the thing was and gasped with horror.

It was a giant box crusher.

"Jelly?" came a voice nearby.

Eggs jumped and looked around. The voice had come from the other hanging cage. Eggs stood up to get a better look. A man was hanging upside down in the cage. His hair and beard were long and matted, and his eyes were unusually bright, giving him a thoroughly crazed look.

"When I'm good, I get jelly. I like *jelly!*" the man said.

"Who are you?" Eggs whispered.

"Who are *you*?" the man asked.

"I'm...I...I don't know anymore," Eggs said wearily. He closed his eyes.

"Boy?" came the voice.

Eggs didn't answer.

"Boxtroll?"

Eggs still didn't answer.

"Dressed like a Boxtroll, but looks like a boy," the man said with a wild giggle. "A boy-troll? Or a box-boy? Hmm. Try the Latin—*arca archa puer. Jelly!!!!* A new species unknown to science! New and improved! Who did that? You did that. That you did. You made you."

Eggs opened his eyes and looked at the prisoner.

"I did what?" Eggs asked.

The prisoner stared at him very hard, then winked.

"Jelly," he whispered.

Snatcher's sneering voice tore through the darkness behind them.

"The poor father woke. Oh, he cried, cried, cried! All 'cause he forgot to lock his babe inside...." Snatcher sang.

Eggs froze—he even stopped breathing. The world seemed to be reeling with the revelation.

"He's my...You're my...Are you my father?" Eggs asked the prisoner. "They didn't kill you, either!"

"Jelly!" the prisoner responded. Then he began cackling uncontrollably.

"Father!" Eggs called.

"He was once!" Snatcher interjected, and laughed meanly. "You won't get much out of him now, though. A decade hanging upside down scrambled his noodle pretty good. Still, he did a fine job designing my Monster Drill. Best inventor in town, your dad. Working with the best little builders."

He gave the stack of Boxtrolls a kick.

"But the filthy beasts have served their purpose," Snatcher continued. "Time to crush 'em. Are you ready, Mr. Trout?"

"Just a few more to add to the pile, boss!" Trout replied.

"Why?" shouted Eggs. "Why would you do this?"

Snatcher gazed up at Eggs.

"Fair question. See, Portley-Rind and his ilk, they might need a bit of convincing. I'm going to have to show them I've really exterminated all the Boxtrolls. So think of me as a hunter presenting his pelts. Proof of a job well done."

"No!" Eggs screamed wildly.

"You can yell all you want, boy. But you've seen it yourself. These Boxtrolls aren't going to run."

Eggs winced.

"I know," he whispered.

As more Boxtrolls were placed on the pile, Eggs could see they were all trembling in terror. Tears spilled down Eggs's face, but he couldn't look away. They were his family. They were all he had.

"Make way, men! I want to pull the crushing lever myself!" Snatcher called. He gave Eggs an ugly grin. "It's the little moments that mean the most."

Snatcher headed for the crushing machine. Eggs sat down heavily in his cage and buried his face in his hands.

"It's over...." he whimpered.

The prisoner began chuckling.

"You made you," he said.

"Why do you keep saying that?" Eggs asked. "What did I do?"

"You made you," he repeated.

He was staring very intently at Eggs. Something in the man's eyes made Eggs feel he might not be as crazy as he seemed.

"You did it," the man said, pointing at the pile of Boxtrolls. "Tell them."

"I tried. They won't listen. They're scared, and they can't change who they are," Eggs replied.

"You can do it. You made you. You made you."

Eggs racked his brain, trying to understand what the man was telling him. He looked down at the trembling pile of Boxtrolls.

Why not give it one more try? Eggs thought. *What do I have to lose?*

"Fish! Shoe! Everyone, listen! You *can* do it. Because…I did it. I'm a Boxtroll, too, but I left the cavern! I took off my box and stopped hiding, and that means you can do the same thing. Just stand up and take the first step!"

The Boxtrolls seemed to have stopped shivering. Were they listening to him?

"All you have to do is get out of your boxes and put one foot in front of the other."

Eggs banged the bars of his cage loudly.

"Please. Do it for me! Please!"

There was silence. None of the Boxtrolls were moving.

"Well, good speech," Snatcher called cheerfully. "Wish I could hear it again, but I've got some boxes to crush. Three, two, one!"

Snatcher flipped a giant lever. Eggs threw his arms over his eyes. There was a bone-chilling, sickening crunching sound. When Eggs opened his eyes, the pile of boxes had been flattened into the ground.

"NOOOOOOO!!" Eggs screamed, shaking with sobs.

"Okay, men, load 'em up!" Snatcher called.

The Red Hats began tossing the flattened boxes into the cab of Snatcher's giant drill. Eggs hugged his knees and sobbed bitterly.

"Look what you did. Look what you did," said the prisoner.

"What do you mean? I didn't do anything! I failed!" Eggs sobbed.

"Look what you did. Look what you did," he kept repeating.

"The monsters are all loaded up in the Mecha-Box, boss," called Trout.

Snatcher stared up at Eggs, giving him an ugly look.

"All but one," Snatcher growled.

Eggs watched in horror as Snatcher waltzed toward his cage.

"No..." Eggs whispered.

"*Oui!*" Snatcher said in his Frou Frou voice. "Let's put on a leetle show! Costumes! Makeup!"

One of the Red Hats grabbed Eggs through the bars and crammed a Boxtroll mask over his head. Snatcher howled with laughter.

The Mecha-Box powered up with a series of whirls and whines. Hatches slammed shut. The world rumbled as the machine began to crawl across the factory floor and out a massive set of double doors.

The cavern was left in darkness and silence, save for a single voice.

"Look what you did."

Chapter 17

Winnie was having a very bad dream about an earthquake when the sound of a voice blaring over a loudspeaker awakened her.

"Hear ye, hear ye! A new day is dawning! Come out of your homes, good citizens of Cheesebridge! The curfew has been lifted."

Winnie sat up slowly, the blood draining from her face.

"Oh, no," she said. "Please don't let this mean what I think it means."

She quickly dressed and ran down the stairs and out the front door. Standing on the Cheese Guild's front steps, Winnie could see that all over Market Square, people were emerging from their homes. An enormous machine was rolling across the square toward the Cheese Guild, and riding it like it was some kind of horse was Snatcher himself. He talked into a gadget that broadcast his voice through a loudspeaker on the machine.

"Fear not!" he announced. "The monsters have been vanquished!"

Winnie stopped in her tracks and pressed her hands to her stomach. She felt as if she might be sick right there.

"Join me! I am the purger of your pests! I am the white knight who has taken back the night!" Snatcher boasted.

A small crowd had gathered and was following the lumbering machine, parade-style.

So he really did it, Winnie thought, fighting back tears. *He killed all the Boxtrolls. Oh, poor Boxtrolls! Poor Eggs!*

A fellow wearing a one-man-band contraption joined the crowd. Snatcher pointed at him.

"You there! Play something celebratory!" Snatcher ordered. "I've just exterminated an entire species!"

The one-man band obliged, striking up a cheerful tune as Winnie made an exclamation of disgust.

"That despicable, monstrous, deceitful Red Hat!" she said, wiping away tears.

Deceitful.

Indeed, Snatcher was the most deceitful human being Winnie had ever known. Was it possible, even just remotely, that Snatcher was being deceitful now, too?

Maybe he's lying, she told herself. *Maybe there's still hope!*

The procession had almost reached the Cheese Guild's steps.

Snatcher trilled into the loudspeaker, "Oh, Lord Portly-Riiiiind! I come bearing the most delightful news!"

The door behind Winnie opened, and her father brushed past. He blinked in amazement at the giant machine, and the crowd, and the triumphant Snatcher.

"Snatcher, what is that thing?" Winnie's father demanded, pointing at the machine.

"Oh, this old thing?" Snatcher said, blinking rapidly à la Madame Frou Frou. "Why, it's simply the brilliant creation I used to deliver our fair town from its pest problem forever. As advertised." He tipped his hat.

The crowd burst into applause.

"That's quite the claim," Lord Portley-Rind said, looking skeptical. "Can you prove it?"

Snatcher gave him a reptilian smile.

"I thought you'd never ask. Boys, show him!"

The Red Hats scurried forward and deposited a stack of flattened boxes at the bottom of the stairs. They fanned them out like a gory welcome mat.

Winnie pressed her hand over her mouth.

"No," she whispered.

The crowd was gasping and murmuring excitedly. Lord Portley-Rind looked positively astonished.

"Your Lordship, I promised you that I would not rest until I caught the very last Boxtroll, and as you can see, I am a man of my word," Snatcher declared.

He flipped a switch on the Mecha-Box, and a mechanical arm swung around, displaying a chain, from which dangled Eggs, who was decked out from head to toe in a Boxtroll costume.

"What? No!" shouted Winnie, but the excited and alarmed crowd drowned out her voice.

"Fear not! The monster is safely restrained. He is all that remains of the foul Boxtroll hordes!"

"Eggs!" Winnie screamed.

"With this Boxtroll," Snatcher continued, "I will end their reign of terror. I give you peace! I give you freedom! I'd say that deserves a white hat, wouldn't you?"

The crowd cheered wildly.

"A white hat for Snatcher!" someone yelled.

"Be-hatify him already!" called another.

Lord Portley-Rind shifted uncomfortably from one foot to the other.

"Yes, well, I'm not sure. It's a complicated business. There'd have to be a vote, and a shipping order, and paperwork—oh, lots and lots of paperwork," he said hurriedly.

"White hat! White hat! White hat!" the crowd chanted.

Snatcher bowed to the crowd, then turned to Lord Portley-Rind, his arms flung wide.

"Yes, yes, all right. I suppose I must have an extra one lying around here somewhere...."

"Oh, no!" Snatcher said. "Methinks a deed of this magnitude deserves something a bit more...significant. I want *your* hat, Portley-Rind!"

"Preposterous!" thundered Lord Portley-Rind.

Winnie was waving at Eggs, trying to get his attention. But he didn't seem to see her. It was impossible to tell with that mask pulled down over his face, and his head hanging down like that. As if all the fight had gone right out of him.

He must be terrified, she thought.

"Preposterous?" repeated Snatcher, leaning toward the crowd. "My good friends, what do *you* think?"

A chorus of voices erupted.

"Just give it to him!"

"He earned it!"

"Yeah, just hand it over!"

"He's liberated us—give him the hat!"

Looking grim, but realizing there was no way out of it, Lord Portley-Rind nodded.

"Fine," he said through gritted teeth. "As soon as that last Boxtroll is dead, you may have...have...my...hat."

Snatcher squealed with glee like a little girl.

"Oh, I just *knew* you'd come round!" he exclaimed. "Let us proceed with the execution!"

"No! Stop him! Someone stop him! Have you all lost your minds? That's the Trubshaw child. This is *murder!*" Winnie screamed, lunging forward and shoving her way through the crowd.

"Burn the beast! Burn the beast!" the crowd chanted.

Snatcher hit a button and a door in the Mecha-Box slid open, revealing the glowing red metal and flames of the furnace that powered it. Snatcher climbed out of the cockpit and lowered himself to the ground on one of the machine's arms. He handed to Trout a small box with several buttons and a long antenna.

"Gentlemen, do the honors. I have a *hat* to receive."

"*Hat!*" exclaimed Gristle, nodding his head.

Pickles and Trout were exchanging nervous glances. Winnie was just feet from them now.

"I thought this was all gonna be a show, like the Frou Frou thing," she heard Pickles say to Trout. "I didn't know he really meant for us to do it."

"This really does stretch the limits of the term *hero*," Trout agreed. "Didn't we always agree we'd stop if it wasn't fun anymore?"

Gristle caught Trout's last remark and snarled something threatening and unintelligible. Trout gulped.

"Or we could do as we're told," he added.

Looking unhappy, Trout swung Eggs closer to the mouth of the furnace.

"Heat him up! Heat him up!" the crowd chanted.

"Stop it! Don't!" Winnie yelled. "It's murder!"

Gristle laughed and rubbed his hands together.

"I'm enjoying this!" he announced.

Winnie looked back at the Cheese Guild.

"Father! Father!" she screamed.

But her father was scowling as Snatcher spoke rapidly and excitedly to him, and he stared fixedly in the other direction.

"Trout!" Snatcher bellowed. "Lower the beast into the furnace! Musician, drum roll, please!"

"Lower the beast! Lower the beast!" the crowd sang.

A drum roll began as Snatcher removed his red hat, sent it sailing into the crowd, then lowered himself on bended knee before Lord Portley-Rind.

"Oh, very well. Repeat after me. With this hat, I, state your name..."

"With this hat, I, Archibald Penelope Snatcher..."

Winnie turned back to face Pickles and Trout. They had moved the cage a little closer, but their distressed expressions clearly indicated they did not want to kill Eggs.

Snatcher bent and tried to navigate his head into the white hat Lord Portley-Rind was holding out. But Lord Portley-Rind shook his head and gestured toward Eggs's cage, which was still not in the furnace.

"Move it along, Trout!" Snatcher bellowed. "I have a life of privilege to live!"

"Don't he mean *we*?" asked Trout, looking even unhappier. He began to lower the cage again.

Winnie sprang forward and grabbed his arm.

"No, *stop*!" she cried.

"Can't, miss," Trout said, pointing at Snatcher. "Apologies."

"We're just doing our jobs," Pickles added.

"Your *jobs*?" Winnie shouted. "Are you pest exterminators or evil henchmen?"

Pickles gasped with dismay.

"I told you people might think of us that way," he said to Trout, looking deeply hurt.

"You don't have to do this," Winnie pleaded. "You can go from henchmen to heroes!"

Trout halted the descent of the cage.

"You know, she has a point, Mr. Pickles," he said. "This could be our big shot at redemption!"

"Everyone loves a good redemption story," Pickles replied.

"We're flawed, but people love a flawed hero!" Trout said excitedly.

"Yes, sure, we totally do. Just let him go!" Winnie said urgently.

Trout handed the remote to Winnie. She was trying

to figure out which button would lift Eggs up and away from the furnace when someone loomed up behind her.

"Got it!" Gristle roared, grabbing the remote control out of her hands.

"No!" Winnie screamed. She turned to Pickles and Trout. "Do something!"

Trout shook his head remorsefully.

"Sorry, miss," he said. "We may be good guys deep down…"

"But Gristle definitely *ain't*," finished Pickles. "Rotten to the core."

"I am a reprehensible person!" Gristle shouted with pride.

In desperation, Winnie turned back toward the Cheese Guild steps.

"Father, *please*!" she screamed.

But Lord Portley-Rind was too busy trying to keep the white hat off Snatcher's head, while Snatcher kept trying to wiggle his way up under it.

"Quiet, please, for the ceremony of the hat!" Snatcher bellowed.

The crowd instantly fell silent. Lord Portley-Rind sighed.

"With profound esteem for dairy and dairy products, I proudly swear to uphold the dignity of the white hat," Lord Portley-Rind recited tonelessly.

"I proudly swear to uphold the dignity of the white hat," Snatcher repeated.

Lord Portley-Rind squinted and scowled, as if he couldn't remember his next line. As the hushed crowd waited expectantly, Winnie heard a strange noise in the distance. As it grew louder, she realized it was a voice. Shouting a single word over and over again.

"Jelly! Jelly! *Jelly!*"

Gristle spun around, looking for the source of the voice. His mouth dropped open as Snatcher's truck came careering into the square.

Winnie cried out with surprise. To her astonishment, Fish and Shoe were stacked behind the wheel. In the passenger seat sat a pale man with wild hair, a long beard, and strangely familiar eyes.

He was laughing in delight.

Chapter 18

Eggs, look!" Winnie cried, pointing at the truck. "It's Fish and Shoe! They're alive!"

Eggs began to look around. He bobbed his head back and forth, trying to shake the mask loose.

Oh, good, he heard me! Winnie thought. *He knows there's still hope.*

The truck screeched to a stop in the center of the square, and scores of things emerged from the back. For a moment, Winnie didn't recognize the Boxtrolls, because she'd never seen them without their boxes.

"Look!" Winnie yelled. "Boxtrolls. Tons and tons of *Boxtrolls*!"

People began to shout and scream.

"They're nude!" screamed someone.

"It's worse than that—they're *naked*," cried another.

Winnie waved to get her father's attention, but it wasn't necessary. He had seen the Boxtrolls.

"Snatcher! What the devil is the meaning of this?" he thundered.

Snatcher's mouth hung open in disbelief.

"I'm as befuddled as Your Lordship! I crushed those creatures myself!"

Lord Portley-Rind began to turn a shade of red that Winnie knew meant absolute, unfettered rage.

"Archibald Penelope Snatcher, you are a liar, a cheat, and a fraud," Lord Portley-Rind shouted, placing the white hat firmly back on his own head. "That is the closest you will *ever* come to having a white hat."

There was an explosion of squeals and gurgles, and Winnie turned around just in time to see a slew of Boxtrolls swarming over Gristle. Fish emerged from the pile, triumphantly holding up the remote control. Gristle hurled several Boxtrolls to the ground and lunged at Fish.

"Fish, look out!" Winnie screamed. Then she heard a bang, and when the smoke cleared, Gristle was trying to fight his way out of a net. Pickles stood over him, holding the net gun, which made him look…not exactly dangerous, but more threatening than usual, as he jumped up and down on his giraffe-long legs.

"Redeemed!" Pickles announced.

"One hundred percent, Mr. Pickles," Trout agreed, clapping him on the back with one hand and rubbing his own excessive belly with the other.

Fish squealed with delight as he found a button that swung Eggs clear of the furnace. Eggs was wriggling his way out of the Boxtroll costume. With his hands free, he pulled off the mask and tossed it away, then launched himself into the arms of the ecstatic Boxtrolls.

"You're alive!" Eggs shouted. "But how? I saw Snatcher crush you!"

Fish gurgled a mile a minute, adding hand gestures, as Eggs listened with amazement. Winnie pushed her way through the Boxtrolls until she reached Eggs.

"Really? That's incredible," he told them.

Winnie cleared her throat as loudly as she could.

"Winnie!" Eggs exclaimed.

Winnie opened her mouth to say something, then lunged forward and threw her arms around Eggs. Then she stepped back to look at him.

"I'm so glad you're okay," Winnie said. The tips of Eggs's ears had gone quite pink. "And the Boxtrolls, too! What did Fish say? I'm dying to know what happened."

"He says after I begged them to try to get away, they all tunneled down to the bottom box in the back, one after another, and wriggled out. Snatcher never noticed a thing. When the crusher came down, all the boxes were empty!"

"Oh, how brilliant!" Winnie exclaimed.

"You did it! You all got out of your boxes and stood up for yourselves! I knew you could do it," Eggs said, hugging Fish as tightly as possible. "I just knew it."

"Why is that boy hugging a Boxtroll?" yelled a townsperson.

"Are they friends? They can't be—Boxtrolls are monsters!" called a woman.

"Boxtrolls are *not* monsters!" Winnie shouted at them. "They never ate the Trubshaw baby, as you can see for yourselves, because he's right there with Fish and—"

She stopped mid-sentence when she turned to find the wild-haired man standing next to Eggs, who was beaming at him.

"And my father," Eggs said, finishing Winnie's sentence.

"Your *father*?" Winnie asked, her eyes huge.

"Look what you did," Mr. Trubshaw murmured, smiling at Eggs.

"You were right, Father," Eggs said. "They did listen to me. Thank you."

"Jelly," Mr. Trubshaw replied happily.

A murmur was spreading through the crowd.

"Is that Trubshaw?" came a voice.

"Trubshaw the inventor? The baby's father?" called another.

"Trubshaw is alive?" asked a third.

"Snatcher *lied* to us!" a shopkeeper shouted.

Then, suddenly, the whole crowd was yelling and calling Snatcher a liar.

"That's right!" came Lord Portley-Rind's thunderous voice. "Snatcher, you villain, it is time to pay for your lies and the disrespect you paid our beloved Madame Frou Frou!"

Where was he? Winnie and Eggs scanned the crowd. Snatcher was nowhere to be seen.

"Maybe this would be a good time for the Boxtrolls to unflatten their boxes and put them back on," Winnie suggested to Eggs tactfully. Because really, some packages were best left unopened.

The Boxtrolls pounced on the boxes spread out at the bottom of the stairs, and to Winnie's relief, they were all soon re-boxed.

Just as things began to quiet down, a high, shrill voice pierced the air.

"*Excusez-moi*, boys!" cried the voice of Madame Frou Frou.

The crowd turned toward the voice. There, atop the Mecha-Box, was Snatcher.

"*Bonjour*, Portley-Rind! We could have been some-tink special, cherie, *mais non*, you have broken our agreement!" Frou Frou's voice called down, taunting.

"Why is Snatcher talking like Madame Frou—oh," said Lord Portley-Rind, his face turning an alarming red. "Now, this is...awkward. I regret so much."

Snatcher yanked on a lever and the Mecha-Box began moving toward Lord Portley-Rind.

"I'll take my white hat now, or I'll destroy this whole town! Brick by brick and person by person! How do you like me now, *boys*?"

And with a tug on one lever, the machine lumbered forward, all its mechanical arms and tentacles extended and smashing, striking, and crushing everything in its path. Lord Portley-Rind sprinted away from the machine, into the crowd.

"What do we do?" Winnie cried. "If that thing destroyed the Boxtrolls' cavern, it can destroy our town, too!"

And all of us along with it, she added silently.

Had it all been for nothing?

"We can still fight back!" Eggs cried.

To his delight, the Boxtrolls had not run off, and they were not hiding in their boxes. They clustered around Eggs, who gave them an encouraging smile.

"You're not afraid anymore, are you?" he asked.

Fish, who was right next to him, took Eggs by the hand. Eggs grinned. Then they both turned to stare at the Mecha-Box.

"Time to fight back," Eggs said grimly.

"Tima tuh fite beck," Fish repeated.

"Hey! I understood you!" Winnie exclaimed.

"Listen, everyone," Eggs said. "You all built that Mecha-Box. That means you know how to take it apart so it won't work anymore, right?"

The Boxtrolls nodded excitedly.

There was a crash as a leglike appendage from the

Mecha-Box slammed into the ground just feet from them. When the leg lifted, Eggs saw there were several Boxtrolls clinging to it, pulling various parts off and tossing them onto the ground.

"Get your grimy paws off my machine, you vermin!" Snatcher screamed. On the machine's other side, Boxtrolls were stacking themselves and trying to lift the top Boxtroll up onto the Mecha-Box itself. The stack was several feet too short to accomplish this, until a heavyset man stepped forward from the crowd and hoisted the entire stack up over his head.

"We're with you, lads," the big man shouted encouragingly.

"The whole town will be with you," Pickles said. *"People of Cheesebridge! The Boxtrolls need our help! Bring tools, weapons, mechanicals!"*

The response was instantaneous. People ran forward with hammers, wrenches, gears, and bolts. The youngest and strongest lifted the Boxtroll towers to help more and more of the creatures onto the Mecha-Box. One of them hoisted Sparky onto the back of the machine. Holding tight with one hand, he pulled open a control panel and began tearing out wires as the crowd cheered. Oil Can ran back and forth under the machine's feet, squirting puddles of oil in the hopes of making it slip.

"I think they're going to do it," Winnie exclaimed. "I think the Boxtrolls are actually going to take the Mecha-Box down."

In the cabin, Snatcher was trembling with rage. Suddenly, the white hat was sailing over the crowd. A Boxtroll leapt up, caught it, and handed it to Winnie.

I've got to distract Snatcher so the Boxtrolls can keep taking the Mecha-Box apart, Winnie thought.

"Yoo-hoo, Mr. Snatcher!" Winnie called, waving the hat in the air.

"Give me that, you vile little brat!" Snatcher howled, steering the Mecha-Box toward Winnie.

Uh-oh, Winnie thought, staring with alarm at the massive machine. *Maybe I should have thought my next move through.*

Suddenly, she saw Trout and Pickles running toward her.

"Perhaps we can be of some assistance!" Trout cried.

"Most certainly. I love a good game of Pass the Hat!" Pickles agreed.

Winnie gave them a relieved smile and tossed the hat to Pickles before diving out of the path of the Mecha-Box. Pickles put the hat on.

"So this is what all the fuss is about?" Pickles asked. "How do I look, Mr. Trout?"

Before Trout could answer, there was a crash as one of the smashing arms of the Mecha-Box slammed down just inches from Pickles's head. He tossed the hat to Trout, who tossed it to Winnie, who tossed it back to Pickles, as the Mecha-Box veered back and forth between them.

"It's *mine!*" howled Snatcher as the white hat went sailing into the air again.

Someone jumped up, arms outstretched, and caught the hat.

"*Jelly!*" Mr. Trubshaw announced triumphantly, waving the hat around. Gristle caught sight of it and gave a bellow of rage.

"*Hat!*" he yelled, pushing his way closer to Trubshaw.

Winnie watched the Boxtrolls clinging to the Mecha-Box and wondered how much of it they'd managed to disable. It still seemed to be moving at full speed, and it was heading straight for Mr. Trubshaw.

As it loomed over him, a giant smashing arm unfurled. Gristle shoved the last person aside and came face-to-face with Trubshaw. Trubshaw smiled and plopped the hat on Gristle's head, then dove out of the way. The smashing arm slammed into Gristle, sending the hat sailing into the air again. But before the arm could smash anything else, it suddenly broke off of the Mecha-Box and fell to the ground. Winnie could see Fish and Eggs clinging to the wire above it, just outside the cockpit, grinning triumphantly.

The Boxtrolls cheered wildly. They were making progress!

"Stop destroying my indestructible machine!" Snatcher screamed. He leaned out of the cockpit and began swinging a giant wrench at Eggs's head.

"Eggs, look out! Get off of there!" Winnie screamed. But she knew Eggs would not give up until the Mecha-Box was beaten.

"We don't need to take it apart, we need to stop it!" Winnie cried. "But how?"

"Put it out," came Mr. Trubshaw's voice from just behind her.

"What?" Winnie said, turning to give Eggs's father an anxious look.

"Put out the fire...and the machine will die," Mr. Trubshaw explained.

"But how? Put out the fire with what?" Winnie asked.

"Jelly!" Mr. Trubshaw said. As soon as the word came out of his mouth, he shook his head. "Sorry. I mean *water*."

Water...

Winnie stared intently at the Mecha-Box. At its front, the huge vacuum arm swayed back and forth like an elephant's trunk, sucking up any Boxtrolls that got in its way.

"Water," Mr. Trubshaw said, pointing at the vacuum arm. "Suck it up like jelly! Fire goes *out*."

Suddenly, Winnie understood. The Mecha-Box was powered by its furnace. If the fire went out, the Mecha-Box would go dead.

"We have a plan!" Winnie called out to everyone around her. "That hose—Mr. Trubshaw says we can turn it on Snatcher! But I need everyone's help, Boxtrolls and Cheesebridgians, too."

People milled about, confused, but Mr. Trubshaw leapt up onto a railing. He pointed one hand at the vacuum tube and one hand at a manhole cover in the street. Clinging to the Mecha-Box, Eggs saw his father and instantly understood the plan. Eggs began shouting directions to the Boxtrolls closest to him.

Snatcher could hear Eggs shouting, and he snarled with rage.

"You think *you* can destroy me, Trubshaw baby?" he bellowed. "That you can ruin ten years of meticulously planned planning? I think *not!*"

Eggs flattened himself, reached out, and smacked a lever. The Mecha-Box instantly lurched to one side, causing the vacuum arm to smack the ground. A line of townspeople and Boxtrolls was ready. They grabbed hold of the huge tube, then formed a makeshift conga line to stretch the vacuum as far as possible.

"Boh gah!" Fish shouted, pointing to the manhole cover.

"Right, this way!" Winnie agreed. "Hey, I understood him!"

The line of volunteers followed Winnie and Fish, hauling the end of the massive tube toward the manhole. A large man jumped forward and pulled the manhole cover off. Shoe grabbed the mouth of the vacuum and jumped down into the manhole with it.

"Now, Eggs—*now!*" Winnie and Mr. Trubshaw shouted in unison.

Snatcher had pulled a cane from the cockpit of the Mecha-Box and was swinging it wildly at Eggs.

I'm going to have to time this perfectly, Eggs told himself.

Just as the cane whizzed past his head, Eggs dove for the controls, smacking the vacuum lever into the Intake position.

Then he stared in disbelief. Nothing happened.

The plan hadn't worked.

Chapter 19

"What's wrong? What happened?" Winnie cried.

Mr. Trubshaw ran forward and peered into the sewer, where Shoe was still dangling from the tube and dragging it down with his weight.

"Too short!" he exclaimed. "Everyone must pull on the hose as hard as they can! Everyone!"

There was a sudden loud shriek from a Boxtroll who realized several of them were *standing* on the tube.

"*Blepp gloff!*" he cried, and the culprits leapt clear of the tube, which instantly stretched out farther.

On the Mecha-Box, Eggs cringed. Snatcher had lifted his cane again and was preparing to bring it down on Eggs's skull.

"You should have stayed underground, you filthy little monster," Snatcher sneered.

"I'm a boy *and* I'm a Boxtroll! *You* are the monster!" Eggs declared.

The hose still hadn't reached the water.

"Joining in the effort!" shouted Pickles, running to pick up the hose.

"Giving it everything I've got," called Trout, grabbing part of the hose himself.

"Okay, again! *Pull!*" Winnie hollered.

"*Jelly!*" Trubshaw shouted suddenly, flashing a thumbs-up.

On the Mecha-Box, Snatcher had frozen.

"Me? *A monster?*" Snatcher hissed, rearing back and raising the cane high in the air to deliver a crushing blow.

There was a loud sucking sound like someone getting to the bottom of a thick milkshake with a straw. The tube went fat and stiff as thousands of gallons of water shot up it and into the guts of the Mecha-Box. A massive cloud of steam exploded into the air with a deafening hiss. Eggs was blasted clear off the Mecha-Box and bounced painlessly off the top of a vendor's tent before landing on his feet in the square.

With a series of agonizing squeals and pops, the Mecha-Box began to slow and shudder.

"We did it!" Eggs shouted. His voice seemed to echo at the other end of the square.

"We did it! We did it!" boomed other voices.

The crowd turned to see three White Hats rolling the Party Havarti toward the Cheese Guild.

"We did it!" Langsdale repeated. "We got the cheese out of the river....Oh, my."

The White Hats realized that Market Square was a smoking, rubble-filled war zone. They stopped rolling the cheese and stared up at the hissing, smoking Mecha-Box.

"Uh...Lord Portley-Rind?" Langsdale called, squinting and trying to see through the clouds of steam.

"What's happening?" called Lord Boulanger from his wheelchair. "I've gone blind, I've gone deaf! I can't see a thing! What?"

The Mecha-Box made a groaning sound and listed to one side. The weight of the massive drill was enough to carry it over. It came down with a crash as the White Hats dove out of the way, Langsdale managing to pull Lord Boulanger's wheelchair with him.

SPLAT!

The ruined Mecha-Box had landed directly on the Party Havarti, sending missiles of shredded cheese into the air. Lord Portley-Rind, who had finally gotten his white hat back, watched the mess with a look of dismay. The crowd was greatly cheered by the sight of the cheese and began to clap and howl. People pulled big globs of cheese off one another and stuffed them into their mouths. The cheese began to ripple and squirm as if it were alive. Then a cheese-covered figure struggled out of the blob. It was Snatcher, who had landed directly in it. He staggered away from the cheese, and Winnie lost sight of him.

We did it, Winnie thought, looking around. *Working together. Boxtrolls and people.*

She opened her mouth to call Eggs's name, when a fat, squishy hand clapped over her face from behind. Winnie shoved it away, but she could not escape the tight grasp on her arm. She screamed with all her might. Eggs spun around and saw her.

"It's Snatcher! He's got Winnie!" Eggs cried.

Snatcher, who seemed to be rapidly swelling to twice his normal size, lurched toward Lord Portley-Rind, dragging Winnie with him.

"Winifred!" Lord Portley-Rind shouted.

"Giff me mah hath!" Snatcher hissed.

Lord Portley-Rind pulled the hat from his head and lunged forward, holding it out to Snatcher.

"Take it! Take the hat, take whatever you want— just let go of my daughter!" he called. "Winifred, be brave! Stiff upper lip! I won't let that villainous cur take you from me!"

Snatcher's swollen, sweaty hand completely covered Winnie's mouth and some of her nose, but her ears were working just fine. When she heard her father's words, her knees went weak with disbelief and joy. She had played out this moment in a hundred different fantasies—almost plunging to her death from a cliff, almost drowning in a boating accident, almost losing her life in a burning building, almost being dragged to the Death Cave by a monster—and each time her fantasy ended the same way. Her father, distraught and desperate, calling to her to hang tight, because he would save her. Because he loved her.

And now it had actually happened.

He does love me! More than his white hat, more than his cheese, more than anything!

Snatcher grabbed the hat with his hideous, sausage-plump fingers, but when Lord Portley-Rind reached for Winnie, Snatcher hauled her back. He smashed the hat onto his now strangely misshapen head and tried to smile, giving himself a hideous jack-o-lantern face.

"Ha! Now all bow down to Arshiball Snassher," he lisped.

"Gentlemen, comply!" Lord Portley-Rind snapped, dropping to his knees.

Snatcher howled with laughter, and the harder he laughed, the tighter his grip on Winnie's neck. Eggs noticed with horror that her face was beet red.

He's going to choke her to death! Eggs thought.

"Snatcher!" Eggs shouted.

Snatcher peered around with eyes now swollen into little slits.

"Over here!" Eggs said. "Aren't you forgetting something? You said when you finally got your white hat you were going to sit on velvet cushions and eat the finest cheeses in the world. Didn't you?"

Snatcher nodded, suspicious.

"But you're giving up before even setting foot in the Tasting Room?" Eggs said.

"Yeth, of courth," Snatcher wheezed. "Porrlee-Rah, yaw cheethe is mahn!"

"What are you doing?" Lord Portley-Rind hissed to Eggs.

"Saving Winnie," Eggs replied. "Trust me."

"All right," Lord Portley-Rind called, running up the Cheese Guild steps. "Follow me—I'll open the door for you."

Snatcher lurched up the steps like the hunchback of Notre Dame. Winnie gave Eggs a terrified look as Snatcher dragged her inside the Cheese Guild. Eggs ran up the stairs after them, skidding to a halt in the main hallway, just outside the Tasting Room door.

Snatcher was going wild, pulling out cheese after cheese from the cabinets and tossing them onto the table.

"Tathting time!" he yelled. *"White hath, now thit down!"*

Lord Portley-Rind urgently signaled to his men to enter the room.

"Do as he says," he told them.

Bewildered, and more than a little grossed out by the sight of Snatcher, the White Hats took their seats around the table.

"Now we eat cheeth like poppah gennelmen," Snatcher commanded.

"Oh, then you must start with the very strongest cheese!" Eggs called to Lord Portley-Rind, emphasizing his words with a significant nod.

"Uh, yes, of course," Lord Portley-Rind said, masking his bewilderment as best he could. He summoned the butler and pointed to a glass case with a giant padlock. The butler nodded, unlocked the case with a key that hung from a chain around his neck, and placed a box on the table. Lord Portley-Rind lifted the lid and removed another, smaller box, also held shut with a padlock. That one was unlocked as well, and Lord Portley-Rind reverently placed his hand on top of it.

"*Gimme!*" Snatcher said.

"Now, hold on," Sir Broderick interrupted. "That's a rare curd, indeed. The most potent cheese on the Continent."

"Indeed, only the most robust, iron-bellied gentleman can stomach it," Langsdale added.

"All true," Lord Portley-Rind said. "It's made from milk aged in the mummified stomach of a mammoth in a sulfur cave that is only accessible by man for twenty minutes out of every year. Are you, eh, quite sure you can handle it?"

"Of courth," Snatcher said, looking as offended as someone with an elephantine marshmallow for a face could look.

Lord Portley-Rind opened the box. Instantly, the White Hats began to cough and sneeze. Eggs was hit with a wave of smell so hard, it made his stomach spasm, and his eyes burned from the fumes. Winnie staggered backward and dove clear of Snatcher just as her father reached into the box and placed the cheese on the table—a tiny, bumpy green thing that looked like a booger.

"Winnikins!" Lord Portley-Rind exclaimed, grabbing hold of his daughter. "Oh, my Winnikins, you're safe!"

Winnie beamed up at her father.

"Shush!" Snatcher shouted. "Thith ith mah dethtiny!"

"Wait!" Eggs called, seeing Winnie safely out of Snatcher's grip and in her father's arms. "Don't do it, Snatcher. It won't change who you are. Don't eat that. It will make you very sick, or quite possibly kill you."

Snatcher, swollen from head to toe from his full-cheese immersion, turned his hideous swollen face toward Eggs.

"Cheese, white hats, they don't mean anything. They don't make you," Eggs said. "*You* make you!"

Snatcher hesitated for a moment, then glowered.

"I have made *me*, boy," he growled. Then he popped the cheese into his mouth.

The White Hats let out a collective gasp.

"Everybody under the table, *quick!*" Eggs yelled, ducking behind the door and covering his head with his hands. "He's gonna blow!"

"Thith ith really—"

Snatcher's voice was silenced by a loud, wet explosion and what sounded like shovelfuls of pudding hitting the walls and ceiling.

When the worst of it seemed to be over, Eggs slipped and slid along, colliding with Winnie.

"There you are!" Eggs said with enormous relief. "Let's get you out of here."

"Definitely," Winnie said weakly.

Eggs helped Winnie outside and down the Cheese Guild steps.

"It's all over, folks!" Eggs called to the crowd. "Snatcher has left the building! Forever!"

A great cheer spread through the square. People clapped their hands, and Boxtrolls drummed their boxes.

"I must look a fright," Winnie said, looking down at her dripping, torn dress. To her surprise, her father's mangled white hat lay on the steps, just by her feet. She leaned down and picked it up.

"Father's hat," Winnie said. "Who can believe all this happened over a silly hat? Father will want it cleaned—it's got strange stuff all over it, blobby things…looks like…"

"Jelly," came two voices in unison.

Winnie looked up at Eggs, standing straight and tall next to his father, whose eyes gleamed and twinkled at her.

"Yes," Winnie agreed, smiling. "Jelly."

Epilogue

Winifred Portley-Rind stood front and center on a stage set up in the middle of Market Square. A mass of townspeople and Boxtrolls gathered around the stage to listen, enraptured.

"And there I stood in the hideous, clammy grasp of Snatcher, until my noble father served him the cheese that would become his own demise," Winnie declared. "Within moments of putting that priceless cheese in his foul mouth, Snatcher went *ker-boom*! And the rest, as they say, is history. One year ago this very day, ladies and gentlemen. Happy first Trubshaws' Day!"

The crowd clapped and whistled.

Pushing close to the stage, Eggs tried to get Winnie's attention.

"Not now," Winnie whispered. "I've still got to tell the story of the Boxtrolls in the Crusher of Doom!"

"But where's Fish?" Eggs asked.

Winnie shrugged an apologetic "I don't know."

"I'll find you after the show," Winnie said. Then she turned her attention back to the audience.

Eggs slipped around the back of the stage and walked up the cobblestone street. It looked much the same as it had a year ago, except for some new businesses. Oil Can's FixIt Shop seemed to be doing especially good business. And as usual, there was a small line at Sweets's Softee Ice stand, right next door to Sparky's Scrap Shack.

But still no sign of Fish.

He passed Pickles and Trout (or was it Trout and Pickles? Eggs could never remember which was which). They were cheerfully sweeping up the street.

"Afternoon, Mr. Eggs Trubshaw!" Pickles called.

"Ain't it nice and tidy?" Trout added.

"Very tidy," Eggs said. "Have you two seen Fish?"

They shook their heads in unison, never stopping their sweeping for a moment.

"Thanks anyway," Eggs said, continuing up the street.

Eggs heard the rumble of an engine, and then a horn honked.

"Eggs!"

Eggs spun around and spotted the truck. At last! He waved happily at Fish and his father, who was driving. It hardly looked like the same vehicle Snatcher and his Red Hats had once used to patrol the streets and capture Boxtrolls. In place of the chair on the roof of the car, Mr. Trubshaw had bolted Eggs's Music Machine. And the Red Hat logo had been painted clean over, replaced with a silhouette of a Boxtroll and three arrows making a circle—a reminder to all to reuse their junky-bits rather than throw them away.

"I've been looking everywhere for you!" Eggs cried as Mr. Trubshaw pulled the truck over to the curb. "Look what I found! A brand-new copy with no scratch!"

Eggs held the record up for them both to see. It was their favorite—Quattro Sabatinos. Fish gurgled with delight.

"Brilliant, son!" exclaimed Mr. Trubshaw. "Let's give it a spin!"

Eggs tore the paper off the cardboard cover, balled it up, and tossed it into a nearby garbage can. The can made a small noise, then Shoe popped out.

"Shoe!" Eggs exclaimed. "Sorry, I didn't know you were in there. Find anything good?"

Shoe climbed out of the garbage can and waddled over to the truck as Mr. Trubshaw reached up to put the new record on the Music Machine. Gurgling, Shoe reached into his box and handed a grimy, torn thing to Eggs. Then he waddled off down the street, toward the next garbage can.

Eggs stared at the thing, perplexed. It didn't look like the kind of junky-bit Shoe or any other Boxtroll usually picked up. This thing didn't look like it had ever served any purpose.

And yet, as the sound of the Quattro Sabatinos began blaring merrily from the Music Machine, Eggs felt there was something familiar about the object. He fingered a bit of shredded ribbon on the thing, and when the sun caught it for a moment, he saw two letters: PR.

It's Lord Portley-Rind's white hat! Eggs thought, amazed.

"What did Shoe find, son?" asked Mr. Trubshaw. "Anything good? Something we can use in the shop, or for parts?"

"'Fraid not," Eggs said. "This thing is totally useless."

"Brilliant," Mr. Trubshaw said. "Then hop in. I do love taking a nice drive while listening to music. Ah, I've missed listening to the Quattro Sabatinos. I've missed so much. What do you say, son? Shall we be on our way?"

Mr. Trubshaw's expression was eager and relaxed, his hair and beard now only the tiniest bit wild after being cut and conditioned and smoothed for Trubshaws' Day in Cheesebridge's fanciest salon. And as always, the sight of Fish, nodding his head and tapping his box in time to the music, filled Eggs's heart. His two favorite people, who loved him best in the whole world. Only a year ago, humans and Boxtrolls had been enemies, one hunting the other. Now they lived in harmony, side by side.

Eggs tossed the hat back into the trash. He smiled at Fish and at his father.

Then he climbed into the truck and squeezed into the seat between them, and the truck began to move just as Eggs's favorite song started to play. It was all perfect, as if their lives until now had been a story, neatly tied up in a happy-ending bow.

And there was nothing wrong with a happy ending, Eggs thought. Because no matter how often you used one, it never got old or stale or outdated. It worked every single time.